JAGGED ICE

MAINE MAULERS HOCKEY SERIES BOOK 2

ZOE BETH GELLER

KINKY INK PUBLISHING

You can also visit me on Facebook and Amazon.

Please visit my website at zoegellerauthor.com

❀ Created with Vellum

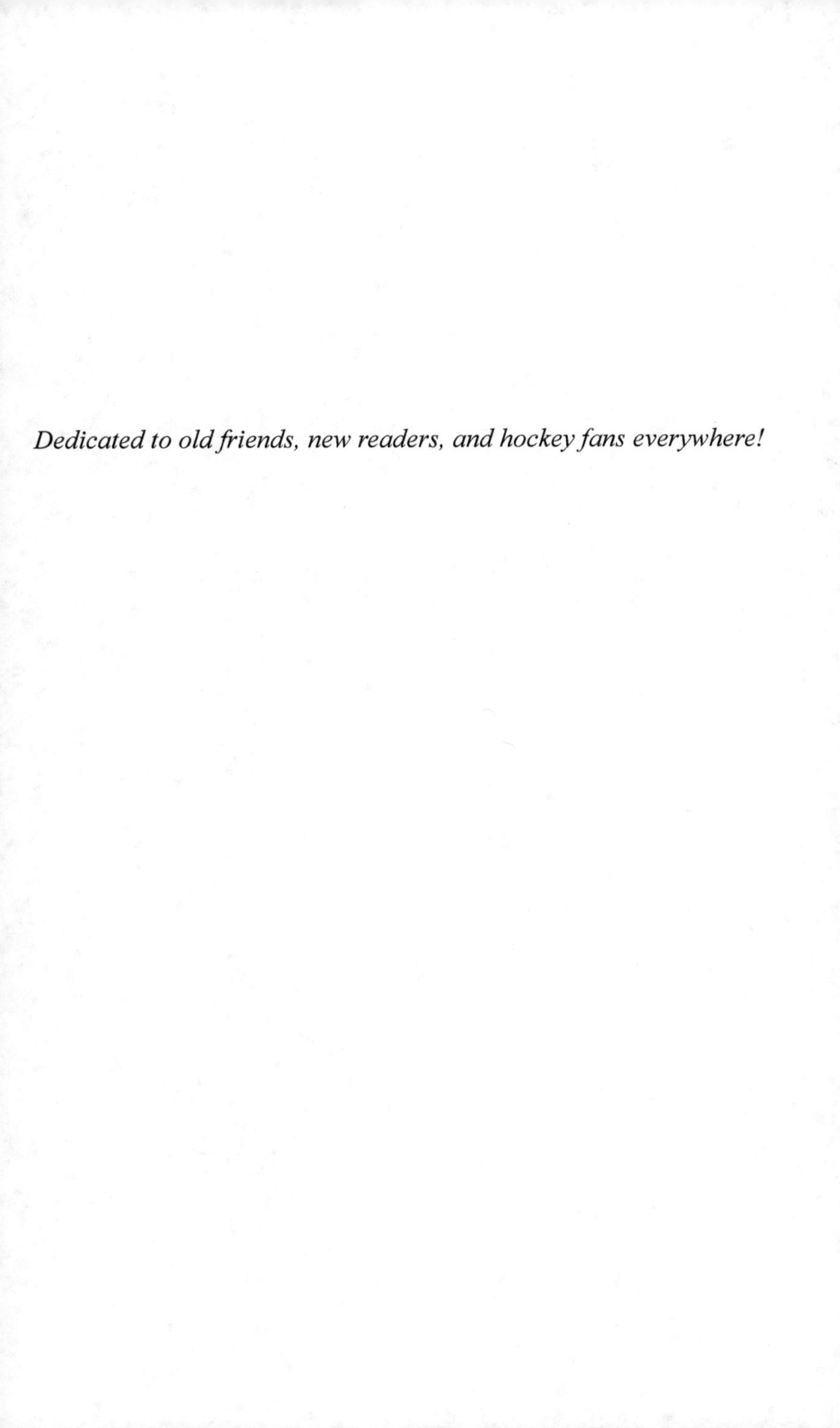

Dedicated to old friends, new readers, and hockey fans everywhere!

PLAYLIST

Playlist for Jagged Ice

High Hopes-Panic at the Disco
It's a Long Way to the Top (If Ya Wanna Rock)-Ac/DC
Love Lies (With Normani)-Khalid Normani
We're Not Gonna Take It- Twisted Sister

1

ALEXANDRE

I can't believe we drank so much, and we only have three days before we head into the playoffs.

I'm lying.

I can believe we drank that much. It's what we do when we all hang out at Hannigan's on the Bay, our neighborhood bar in Maine, and conveniently not far from the arena. They are famous for their craft beer as well as fried cheese balls with jalapeños.

We clinched our wild card slot right before the end of the season. And by barely, I mean, I even held my breath for a minute, and we all ran out of breath racing up and down the ice to get there. We always have to keep our feet moving as quickly as possible and never let up. That's what wins championships.

Winning the last game of the season 2-1 kept me on edge until the buzzer sounded. I hate Overtime. It's nerve-wracking, and there's no telling who will lob a puck into the net first. There's so much fucking weird shit that happens during a game. It's amazing that we don't knock each other out more often— a bloody nose is the least of our worries.

Fistfights due to frustration, paybacks, or just good ole fashion crashing into one another because we're going twenty-two miles an hour on a skating rink two hundred yards long.

Sound insane? Yes.

I think it helps most of us are flawed individuals who have bonded together tighter than a compressed coil. But that was last night, and now I wake up with this morning's leftovers. Namely, a hangover and some random is in my bed.

I swing my toned legs with large thighs, thighs larger than most girls' waistlines, over the side of my humongous bed. The sun sneaks through the blackout curtains I forgot to close, making it impossible to sleep because everything shines like it's been brushed with the gold from a Rolex watch.

We all take naps before our evening games, so the curtains are more of a necessity than me just being lazy and wanting to sleep away the morning. They are no less important than caffeine or energy drinks before a game.

"Mm."

I hear the woman rustle behind me as I head toward the master bathroom large enough to fit the team. One of the perks of a multi-million-dollar house with over four thousand square feet and every toy imaginable.

Damn if I can remember her name. Julie, Jill? The day I remember a girl's name is the day I'm in trouble. I usually call them Mary or something else, whatever springs to mind. I'm always corrected, but it keeps me single, and I enjoy the life of a bachelor as much as I love having money.

Slowly I run my hand through my hair-hair, which oddly reminds me of milk chocolate. Ironic as it is disturbing because I don't care for any chocolate unless it's in a sports drink mixed with liquor.

"Wakie, wakie," I tease the stranger in my bed as my text alert goes off, so I double back to my nightstand.

Wyatt wants to meet up at the gym for a light workout.

Yep, as soon as Goldilocks gets out of here.

You don't know her name, do you? he teases.

No, if I did, she'd be wearing my ring, you know my rule. No personal interactions, just sex with no strings.

I don't have to remind him. He knows me, even as a young rookie, the kid is very perceptive and does exceptionally well on the ice. I hope his skills will help us in the next few weeks. He reminds me of myself at that age, and even though I'm a prick, I like the kid and took him under my wing as much as I could when he arrived here in February.

A "hm" greets me from the bed again.

Why is she still here?

Shit, she's going to be difficult. This is where I really need a friendly neighbor to crash in on me. However, it's not a possibility. I'm live in a mini mansion in a country club, and I don't know my neighbors, nor do I care to.

"Gotta go." I walk to her side of the bed and slap her ass hard enough to get her attention. She liked it harder last night.

"Okay," she mumbles. "You don't remember my name?" She sits up, pulling the sheet around her breasts, breasts I sucked on only a few hours ago.

"What's that?" I turn to her on my way with a no-shit Sherlock look on my face.

"You never remember a girl's name? Do you?" she repeats.

Did she hear an inside rumor?

"That's the plan, you know the rules." No freaking way am I getting married, and I'm too selfish to have kids. What do these women want from me anyway? A hookup is fantastic, even a few months of it, but then they expect to change me, and it all goes to shit.

I don't know what she's heard however, it wouldn't be the first time I get called out for being an asshole. I'm young and built with plenty of money and playing the game I love—hockey.

"Thank you for last night." I dismiss her and head to the shower.

It's a state-of-the-art shower and it never fails to intrigue me how women continue to expect more from me, as if they are different from any other puck bunny I've picked up over the years. Maybe I'm a glutton for punishment. I step into the hot water.

"You're an asshole." She rushes into the bathroom in a huff as if I've offended her.

"I come with a warning label," I shout over the water teeming over my body grateful for the waterfall of numerous jets hitting me at the same time. I duck my head under it and pretend I'm standing under a picturesque mountainside waterfall in Costa Rica.

There, the water is so powerful it makes my ears pound, so I use it to my benefit today, drowning out her voice, which reminds me of a screeching owl rather than an angry yell. I only hear garbled words as they drift in and out of the shower walls, whereby I hope she gets the hint to leave.

On second thought, I don't know her, and it would be prudent to make sure she's not stealing my jerseys or valuables in a fit of rejection. The only items I can think of which might be in jeopardy is my expensive Invicta watch on the nightstand and cash in my wallet, so I decided to let it ride. The hot water feels good on my tired muscles, and I'm staying put.

I can't hear the front door but assume she's left.

I need to hydrate and get a light workout in to stretch my muscles. The muscles I didn't use much last night, but the ones I'll work extra hard in the weeks coming up.

Muscles tend to tighten on me like vice grips, especially after a game. It can happen anytime, even if I sit in the penalty box for two minutes. Good thing we're used to the discomfort and the pain of nasty hits, bruises, cut lips, and traumatic bruises. We are blocking pucks and throwing our bodies like we're meant to fly.

Yeah, crazy ass shit.

And it's a long road to the Cup.

Summer is coming. I can't wait to enjoy Maine's warmer side and make it out to the lakes when they aren't frozen for a change. Not to mention all the yummy lobster. And tote the Cup with us, of course. I'm sure we'll find a new experience for it to endure. I'll have to think of something to go in the record books.

I need to decompress today with the guys and have a light workout before I can begin to think about our game against the Boston Sharks. They're a tough team, making the playoffs for the past four years. They love to hit and get their licks in, not like I don't either, or my teammates, for that matter.

For the next few days, we'll be sitting in meetings where analysts have studied the other team for precisely this moment. They discuss late-night meetings with our coach and those from our specialty units who will arrive at a strategy to use against our opponent. Until then, we will have a day off.

We've never been in the playoff series before, so we're stoked about our first game. I couldn't care less about winning the President's Trophy. It went to Toronto, not Boston, as the number-one team in the entire league. The Trophy has a bad rap as only a handful of teams have gone on to win the Stanley Cup from there.

I'm not crazy about superstitions, but this one is the real deal for me. And even though we've clinched a spot in the playoffs, it's no guarantee we'll make it to the end. Our next step is to beat the Boston Sharks in the first round and win four out of seven games.

We need to get our wins in early. Every team has to win in the opponent's arena.

Our work is just starting as it's a new level of playing and pressure like no other. And we don't have any experience with it except for one veteran player on our team who came in last year to beef up our defense. His name is Colton, and he's the enforcer on the team. We were seriously lacking a man in his position for numerous years. I'm happy he's brought his stellar defense and retaliation hits with him—his essence embodies the change we needed and the one thing we lacked on our D-team.

I do my best as an offensive player as a right winger. Lately, Peety's been coming through in a pinch—yup—he stepped up his game. Maybe he's beginning to hit the height of his career, y'know—found his groove, so to speak.

Glad management got their head out of their ass and got us an excellent defensive player before playoffs. Every team needs a fantastic D-team. I like the newest guy, Colton. I hear he was engaged to an aspiring novelist before he arrived at the end of the season, so he's been fun to add to the weekly group of single guys.

I'm sure he won't mind the camaraderie. Wyatt used to hang out occasionally, but now that he's engaged, he's more apt to head home after a beer or two and forget about an all-nighter unless it's a bachelor party. No one is exempt from that.

Although I wish someone would be our wall to protect us from ourselves when we party, it would ruin the plethora of great stories we've amassed over the years.

The house is quiet when I leave my sanctuary. Throwing on my branded workout gear, I'm a freaking fashion plate as I brew two espressos, down them in one gulp, and head out with my gym bag of hydrating drinks.

Today is a great day to be me, and I want my name on that Cup.

2

CALLIE

Pulling my new Subaru sports utility vehicle into the arena parking lot, I hear the rattle of my kayak strapped to the top, reminding me the weekend is over. It's Monday, and time to be the nerdy girl at work where I'm paid to crunch numbers.

In the world of professional hockey, management, and coaches make up a small pond where everyone knows someone. New blood coming in to manage and coach is a rarity, so the current teams are filled with recycled coaches and old practices, with only a few venturing onto new trends.

Basically, it's a closed system of people who have spent their professional lives working in sports, whether they are proficient at it or not. I marvel at how ironic life can be. After a devastating divorce, a random hookup landed me this dream job just after I finished my master's degree.

I have a good parking spot because I'm the shoe fashionista in the office. Walking the familiar steps across hot pavement, I duck carefully under oak trees, flush with dark green leaves filling in the once bare branches. Chirping birds make a racket as I saunter by on my way to the formidable arena. Bluebirds dive-bomb me as they've wasted no time building nests for their hatching chicks.

The sun comes up earlier here than any other place on the Eastern Seaboard, and the bounce in my step is the endorphins in my body because our team is in the playoffs. I have a hot latte from Luke's in my hand as I enjoy the day's warmth.

Summer makes me smile because I don't have to carry a jacket for the next few months. Entering the elevator for the ride to the third floor, where our operations department awaits, I'm greeted by my bestie, Sarah.

"Girl, no coffee for me?"

"Crap." I grimace. "My bad. Sorry."

She smiles, looking chic in her black with gold trim Coach pumps, and white short-sleeved silk blouse with a black business skirt. No doubt I will find the matching jacket on the back of her chair.

She's the living embodiment of the matching Barbie doll outfits my mom sewed for my dolls when I was a kid. Matchy, matchy, however, it's a sharp look when done correctly, and she wears it well. I envy how she's maintained her figure and looks after having three kids. In heels, she's a statuesque 5'7 and never complains about her shoes hurting her feet.

Fuck me. Who gets that lucky? My feet grow a size bigger if I stand too long, and I don't have kids, not that I'm opposed to having them.

"So, how was your weekend?" she asks, walking me to my office.

"Relaxing, went out on the kayak with Lucy. She loves the water so much— I can't tell who enjoys it more, her or me. I wish I didn't have to hose her off afterward and dry her, but I can't have her lying around on my leather couch."

"Oh, yeah." Sarah nods and wrinkles her nose. "Wet dog smell in the house is bad."

"Yup." My lips make a pop sound like a kid's lips slipping off the end of a sucker.

At the end of the corridor, Sarah pushes the glass door open for me, and we enter the den of analytics. Computers are humming, and people are buzzing.

"What's with the busy bee syndrome going on today? Did I miss anything?"

Checking the Garmin sports watch on my wrist, I'm relieved, I'm on time.

"They are panicking over the June deadline when we have to make our trades, y'know." She shrugs, stopping at my desk and letting me get situated.

"That's normal. Today feels —abnormal."

Matt, my co-worker, pops by. "Hey guys, staff meeting in ten." He hurriedly continues down the hall popping in and out of rooms.

"What the hell?" I murmur.

"I think it has something to do with your report on Peter Czuchry's analytic score putting him in the hot seat for a trade."

"Oooh." It dawns on me, for one sinking moment, I feel bad when we have to pull teammates apart. I understand it's for the greater good and keeps me in a job, but there's always a twinge of guilt or remorse when we have to say goodbye to anyone in our Mauler family.

Sarah pats me on the back, "It's just business," and heads to her desk in front of the Director of Operations office suite.

Hmm, I didn't plan on it happening so fast. I just brought him up last week. I wonder who we might get for him. My moment of reminiscing about a player that's been here his entire career passes as I anticipate getting a good trade for him. He's twenty-eight, which isn't old, in fact, he might have better days ahead of him. I ask myself if I want to gamble on it.

My job is to catch these things so the team can come up with creative trades to strengthen our team. With salary caps, we're all under the gun, and a younger person will be less expensive. Then, maybe we can get a better goalie in camp who has the potential to be an improvement over our current backup.

Even though I work in the building packed with eye candy on the first floor, I rarely see the players. Players and management are polar opposites, like batteries— we repel each other. Naturally, everyone knows this. It's like the Hatfields and McCoy's when they mix in an office setting because one side isn't going to be happy.

But I watch the games, study the team, and run the statistics before submitting reports.

I earn a hefty paycheck to do this. The money goes to my new mortgage after I had to sell the marital home two years ago.

I say I'm still in recovery. Sarah says I'm a chicken shit for not dating, and she's right. Those damn dating apps scare the shit out of me.

I take a swig of my coffee, which is now lukewarm and losing its flavor. Tossing the cup in the trash, I scoop up an armful of reports on my desk and strut across the carpet. My Prada pumps match my kaki high-low trench coat and leggings. The temperature in the office is always cool, but my outfit is hot, and coming from me, that's making a statement.

I have a plan in motion for being single. If I'm not having sex, it's shoes and shopping. I have a thing for S's—sex, shoes, and shopping. The only problem is I might go broke before I have a hot hookup with anyone and have too much shit in my house due to a growing addiction. I need to get laid before I go broke.

3

ALEXANDRE

"Wyatt. Dude." I give him a bro hug, clasping hands and pulling each other in to touch shoulders. We file into the locker room to change and grab some gear to work out. I need to make up for last night's round of shots and far too many beers.

Glancing over my right shoulder – it's Peety bringing up the rear. "Peety, nice game, nice game." That's probably the most my teammates have heard from me in a while. I'm not exactly the gregarious type by any stretch of the imagination, but the high of being in the playoffs for the first time has me stoked.

I'm even excited enough to be—well, jovial. Beyond hanging out to drink after a good game or showing up when the captain strongly encourages me to, it's not my thing to participate in team activities.

"Hey, man." Peety gives me a fist bump, and it looks like he's gone a few rounds with Rocky because he's all sweaty. Maybe he ran here. "Y'know, you all stuck me with the tab last night. If anything, you guys owe me a drink for winning the game for you."

Wyatt chuckles, and I'm unmoved. We know Peety's not really

complaining because we're constantly fucking with each other. To be clear, I can be an asshole.

"Yeah, we just want to keep you on your toes," I reply.

Peety rolls with all the punches, makes jokes—pulls pranks. I hear he's the guy you drink with after a breakup. I've never had my heart broken as an adult, but if I did, he'd be my go-to guy.

I'm surprised he hasn't found his soul mate yet. I'm an asshole, so I don't expect much in the girl department. All I want is listed on a short list of entirely superficial qualities.

Peety is always the last guy off the ice and stays calm on the bench. He never lets us get down even if we're losing—he keeps our spirits up. He's also a great D-man, and he comes through in a clutch, lobbing one into the net when we need it most. Dependable.

I'm not alone in my opinion. Everyone knows he's the sticky glue that keeps us going. Bridging issues between players who may have an issue with each other is a chore, but he's good at it and always finds a way to smooth things over.

Like in January when Luc's little sister played Wyatt. Luc is our goaltender, and between the two of us, we quickly resolve most things. We'd have fixed it if corporate had just stayed out of it. It's just one way they micromanage players.

The upper echelon and the players are never chummy.

Wyatt is a freaking great kid and did not deserve the undo attention. Ultimately, it all worked out, and now he's with his fiancé, Emily. She's older than him, and I'm closer to her age, but they make a great couple.

Given my lack of interaction, I pay more attention to the banter around us than anyone can surmise. When I'm in a shitty mood, everyone knows. I'm selfish that way.

I don't have much restraint when I'm pissed, and my quiet disposition can easily erupt into a cyclone. It's best to avoid all contact when I'm pissed off. There's no telling what might get broken. A few sticks are minor compared to smashing up someone's scooter if it has blocked my car into a spot in a shopping plaza or private airport.

I wouldn't say I like the drama the wives and girlfriends bring into our testosterone-fueled world. As far as I'm concerned, that shit should stay where it belongs—in junior high school. Cat fights are notoriously over guys, giving me another reason to avoid getting serious with anyone.

I prefer to focus my energy on hockey, and I skirt playing defense unless I have to. This year proved to me we can win. If we all do our job on the ice, whether we need to play D or not, and stick with the program, we will be successful. So maybe there is something to team bonding and the coach's game plan.

I'm not sure we're all committed to the new sticking to your zone or sticking to the player—as the case may be. It's hard for us to commit to anything one hundred percent, but we're where we are because we're coming together as a team and committed more than eighty percent of the time to the team this year.

No one can have a perfect season any more than a perfect day.

"Guys, my house tonight. I have the jet skis out, and the ribs have marinated a few days. I have coolers of beer. Come at four," Peety announces in the locker room.

"And you need a girlfriend, but I don't see that happening any time soon," I shout back.

"Work in progress, man, work in progress." He opens his locker, and inside is a very, very cold Smirnoff Ice sitting on the top shelf.

Our Captain, Victor, is big on us doing things together besides throwing a few back. So when Colton and Victor team up with our Alternate Captain, it's an automatic team-building event. We're creating a real family.

"Oh, fuck no! FUCK, you guys!" He slams the locker closed, but not in anger. It's more of an 'Oh, fuck,' they got me. And this is going to SUCK.

I can't help but chuckle. We're being assholes, and we all know it, but the game has to be played. I turn around to watch.

"You guys are the worst!" Peety exclaims, grabbing the ice-cold malt beverage. It's lemon-flavored, and after a few gulps, it hits the stomach hard, like a lead sinker—an hour later, it's more like a bowel cleanser than a good time.

He pops the top, drops to one knee, and chugs.

The guys hoot and laugh. Victor slaps him on the back.

"I'm going to find out who did this and paybacks are a bitch." He stands and tosses the bottle in the closest trashcan as he holds it in the backwash—another fun leftover from being saturated from last night.

"Good luck," Justin, our burly defenseman, scoffs as we grab our healthy drinks, weightlifting gloves, and belts and head to the gym.

Just watching him drink that shit makes me want to hurl.

And we know there are five more of them hidden somewhere.

The gym is filled with half the team, and the goalie is in his special corner working on his polymetric exercises for flexibility and muscle development.

I grab a gym towel from the pile and fuck me if someone didn't plant an Ice there. I wish I could pretend I didn't see it and put the towel back, but that would be cheating. I looked around to see if anyone noticed.

"Ahhh," teases Wyatt, "I saw."

"Fuck off," I snarl, popping the top, dropping to one knee, and chugging the shit. Christ, it's not even noon.

The cold liquid hits my throat, and it's refreshingly cool at first. Then, a slow burn of the citric flavoring kicks in. Brain freeze commences, and my gut feels like a softball sits in it from the carbonation. Then the fun part—the after-taste hits. I stand and toss the empty bottle into a large trash can by the door.

"That's so nasty. It's clear someone is being the joker today," I grumble as I grab the towel embossed with the *Gatorade* logo.

It's hard to believe *Gatorade* was created as a hydration drink in 1965 by the University of Florida. It gave their football team an edge over the competition, and its sales revenue still helps their athletic department.

I watch everything I eat, especially sugar because it's not good for us, so I'm not happy about consuming whatever's in the *Smirnoff Ice*. Heading to the free weights, I guzzle from my bottled water, pop my earbuds in, and listen to *It's a Long Way to the Top* by AC/DC.

An hour later, we're taking showers, and I decide to put an Ice on Peety's phone. When he comes out of the shower, he groans before taking a knee again.

Wyatt opens his gym bag to pull out a bottle of cologne, and I'm on it.

"Who's the bitch now?"

"Fuck, I'm going out to lunch with Emily and her parents, who are visiting, and it would be nice not to smell like a distillery," he jokes.

"Relax, at least you're twenty. That's a respectable age," Peety adds, and as he reaches into his locker for his shoes, there is one in his sneaker.

"Okay, I've had two. Where the hell are the others?"

"Got one here. Guess I picked the right or wrong shower depending on how you look at it," Luc says, coming out with a towel wrapped around his waist with one in his hand.

"Who the hell brought them in any way?" I look around for a suspicious face.

Sean, one of our left wings, can't contain a chuckle, "Okay, you sissies," he pulls one out of the coolers in his bag, drops, chugs, and tosses the empty bottle to me.

"Oh, and you think that gets you off the hook? Eh?"

"No, but it was fun, wasn't it?" He snickers as he fists bumps Wyatt on his way out the door and hollers, "Later," over his shoulder.

"Damn, how did he become so fucking sneaky?" Luc comments while drying off.

I hope to God he doesn't do a fucking helicopter, as goalies are notorious for being a bit unhinged.

"Don't know, but see ya." I'm out the door as my phone vibrates in my black Maine Maulers tracksuit pants pocket.

Normally, I don't answer calls I don't recognize, but it's a local number, and who the hell calls Maine anyway? There aren't enough people in the state to be a target for robocalls from telemarketers.

But then again, is anyone immune to them?

Against my better judgment, I answer.

"Hello?"

"Hi, Alexandre. This is Marty from the Maine Mudders Newspaper, and I was wondering how you feel about the potential trade of your teammate, Pete Czuchry."

"What?"

"Yeah, rumor has it the CORSI numbers show that he's slipping, and the Maulers might trade him." His business tone and confident delivery convince me this isn't a gag.

"Where did you hear this?"

"Can't reveal my sources, man. You know how it is," he says and snickers nervously.

"The hell I do." I hang up. My day is officially ruined as I make an about-face and head to the one place that's off-limits to players as an unwritten rule.

4

CALLIE

"I t's been a long time since we went out," Sarah cajoles me after our staff meeting.

"Um, you're right. I've been a hermit lately." I take a seat behind my desk and pop my laptop screen.

"So, are you going to the playoff games?" She stands and turns on one foot, a bad habit she started to be cute, but now she's doing it so often I'm afraid she'll sprain her ankle.

"Possibly," I pause. "Well, now that this deal with Peter Czuchry might come to fruition, I better make sure the numbers are consistent."

"You mean consistently under par."

"I'm not out to get anyone. I'm one of the few people assigned the task of making sure we've got the best team. Even you get an annual evaluation."

"Hm, well, I think I have more wiggle room." She winks.

"You're a married woman," I remind her. "Get your mind out of the gutter."

"Well…" She glances down the hall toward her boss's office to make sure no one is listening before leaning in to tell me. "My boss is rather cute. Glad I don't work late at night." With that, she gives me a sly grin and sits across from me.

"Sarah, that's terrible."

"I'm human, y'know, married ten years. The hubby is sporting a beer belly, and some of the guys here, let's face facts—are sexy as hell. You can't deny we're sitting three floors above the hottest man candy in the entire state—hell, the entire country." She leans forward and whispers, "It's all right here, underneath you," she grins, "and most of them are at the age when they want to settle down."

"Is that meant to be a hint?"

Leaning back in her chair, she says, "If the shoe fits, wear it."

"I'm comfortable sharing my single life with Lucy."

"A dog is fantastic, but it's not normal companionship, and you shouldn't use your time with her to push a man away," she grimaces, "that's—not so good."

"I know, it's been two years. I should be dating," I concede.

"Right-e-o, take your own advice." She stands, spins on her designer heels, an inch higher than mine, and pauses at the door. "Look, all I'm saying is maybe it's time you give a guy a break. To use a hockey reference, you play defense every time a man approaches you when you go out. You have to move on. Your ex did. I want you to be happy."

"I know."

I get it. It's time to stop sulking and move forward.

The phone on my desk rings, and I answer it.

Sarah waves bye and disappears.

"Oh, hi," is all I can say to my ex-husband on the phone. I'm surprised to hear his voice, a sound I used to listen to every day until it stopped abruptly, leaving me on the floor curled in a ball like a newborn kitten and just as defenseless.

I take a deep breath to not panic—or show I'm still harboring resentment over our breakup and having to sell our house.

"No, I don't know where your leather jacket is. It's been almost two years since our divorce. Why would I have it?" I lie.

I listen to him tell me how he misses it.

Yeah, he should. I spent a fortune on it for our first wedding anniversary. I'm up to my eyeballs in student loans, and he's what? Having a baby? I knew they got married last year, but isn't that quick?

"Well, good luck. Sorry, I can't help you on the jacket."

We hang up, and I feel a bit guilty because I have his jacket. Aside from the wedding pictures and memories, it's the only evidence he was in my life. Funny how it can all be erased so quickly.

He's starting a family, and I must admit I'm jealous. He cheated and gets to have it all, and I am spooning with my dog on cold nights. Well, every night. Lucy is a sweetie, and she gets me.

Certainly, I can move on. It takes a minute for some of us to get over a cheating son of a bitch. At first, I thought it was the long hours I put into getting my master's degree, but when I found out his affair had been going on for some time—let's say it left a mark because I was still madly in love with him.

On a positive note, I wouldn't have ended up here without the divorce. A hookup afterward opened some doors, and the fact I'm from Maine made my position here a no-brainer. Openings in the NHL don't come up often, especially in a state with limited career opportunities.

I loved living in Connecticut. Yale was the bomb. However, all work and no play made me a bad and boring wife.

I spin my chair and stare out the window at the lush green landscape in the distance. I feel as empty as the cloudless horizon with no one in my life and nothing on my mind.

Dating, what a concept. I may work in an environment dominated by men in business and tracksuits, but not many are datable. Sure, there are plenty of single hot players here. I doubt many would ever consider dating me. If my position here doesn't scare them off, my aura of disdain for men, in general, will be enough to repel them.

I'm not old at twenty-seven, but I'm not getting any younger. I should probably stop procrastinating and try to be receptive to a date. Maybe dipping my toes in the pond isn't such a bad idea.

But do I really want to risk losing everything again? The embarrassment I felt when my ex moved on so quickly made me feel less than attractive, and his betrayal gutted me. I don't picture sexy hockey players as being faithful husbands and future daddies to the kids I want. It just seems their playboy lifestyle is counterintuitive for the future I have in mind.

I need air after the phone call. I have to figure out the playoff schedule and hit those games. Although it's not the regular season, I doubt anything will pop up to change the scores I go by because the playoffs are where the game is upped. The players will succumb to the pressure or thrive on it. But I owe it to the team and Peety to continue my due diligence.

Do we have the winning-est team who can grab the Cup this year? The team needs more depth is what we're discussing with the coaches. I think we might be weak in our defense, which is why a defenseman who's more of an enforcer would be helpful.

Being in the playoffs puts us in a great position to make a good trade and get someone who would have turned us down a few years ago. Last year we did well only to crumble toward the end of the season, falling out of our spot next to the top-seeded teams and missing the wild card slot.

Numbers, I tell myself, never lie. I walk out of the office to the girl's bathroom to relieve myself of the coffee I held well past its need to escape. Afterward, I check myself in the mirror while I wash my hands. Noticing a few stray hairs, I use my damp fingertips to push them back into my messy bun. I think my updo looks sexy with this outfit and meets my sole purpose to look more sophisticated.

I'm in my head, still reeling from Mitch's phone call and pissed about how happy he sounds when I'm not. He's got it all and is enjoying life. I tell myself I'm enjoying life, but it's so nice those first weeks of a new crush, the euphoria of the hormones and hot sex that leaves one's body weak afterward.

Yeah, I haven't had anything close to it in so long I've resorted to hot and steamy romance novels and erotica to get off at night. I should be ramping up my game face, not shrinking behind one.

My head is down as I walk with my mind elsewhere when I absentmindedly walk through the glass doors and collide with a massive chest.

Bam.

I would have fallen backward had strong hands not saved me from being caught in the office doors as I'm gently pulled past them to safety. The doors close behind. I can't dismiss the musk scent as it washes over me as gentle as a summer wave on the Florida Keys.

"Wow," I gasp in shock as my collision hit faster than a lightning bolt.

Looking up, I find myself staring into the eyes of the notorious bad boy Alexandre Holloway realizing he saved me from falling on my ass in front of everyone.

That would be an embarrassing move on my part. More so than my divorce nightmare and days of going through tissue boxes I bought at the bulk buying co-op in town.

"Sorry, I guess I was in a rush, too." His sexy deep voice is titillating. It's hard for me to pull my eyes from his gaze. "Are you okay?"

"Um, yeah."

His hands warm me like a sip of brandy and easily slide off me once I'm steady, leaving me with regret. It's been so long since a man has touched me, his touch shakes me.

"Sorry, in a hurry." He charges past me like a man on a mission to save Earth from a meteorite strike.

That's weird, players only come up here if it's something terrible, and even at that, they go to the General Manager's office. No player comes up here to see us.

I'm steady in my heels. I regain my composure, straighten my dressy shirt, a mock trench coat, and continue to the bathroom. I'm curious about a player being on our floor. I want to follow Alexandre to see what's happening, but I realize I'll hear all the details from Sarah later. I pee and make sure my hair is in place before leaving.

Maybe I'm just overcompensating for my lack of a love life. I run my hands over the back of my dress top and make my way back through the infamous doors where I bumped into that hunk of a ladies' man to check out the hot right winger in our office.

I glance towards my desk. He's standing there while guys swarm around him. He seems to be distracted, and I see his face of anger turn into one of acceptance when he realizes he can't escape without being rude.

Guys are shaking his hand. And I notice others using their phones to take snapshots from their desks.

Fuck me— he's drop-dead gorgeous. The hair on the back of my neck rises as I step into my office, brimming with testosterone.

5

ALEXANDRE

I look over the heads of fans packed in this small office and see a woman walking toward me who's hotter than fuck. She carries herself like a dancer, at ease in her high heels, and her long legs go all the way to China. Instead of walking past the office, she comes into it.

Oh shit! This can't be Callie—the woman I stormed up to confront.

Shit.

When she enters the room, the guys scurry away like squirrels who need to hide their nuts. Ironic when you consider we're all a bunch of juveniles' downstairs who never tire of making crass jokes about balls and nut sacks.

My colossal ego prevents me from being offended because everyone left so quickly. With just the two of us in the room, I can focus on Callie. Her dark eyes, prominent and inviting, remind me of Mom's homemade Christmas fudge. Her complexion glows and her long eyelashes are entirely natural. She's not the type of girl I date and definitely not my preferred brunette whom I consider to be my 'type.' There's nothing frail about her, and she's almost as tall as me.

She's a babe if I ever saw one, and trust me, I've had more than my share since being a bachelor is my second gig— if being a toddler on skates counts anyway. I'm not splitting hairs over it.

She's a woman, and no doubt she'll want me, so she'll be a pushover. I should have no problem convincing her Peety needs to stay, and then she can ask me for my phone number. I can handle this, no sweat.

The fans clamoring for an autograph or another story about a 'one-timer' shot in the last game fade away. Or is her presence making me forget my few minutes of fame and adulation?

"You," is all I can think to say because it suddenly dawns on me I bumped into her three minutes ago.

"What?" she asks, unmoved by my physical presence and awesomeness. "What is bothering you, Alexandre?" Brushing past me to get to her desk, her head of warm blonde hair passes beneath my nose, leaving my senses to imagine a crate full of fresh Georgia peaches.

I'm reminded of my favorite dessert of peach cobbler from my childhood when we weren't on the road with hockey. I'm instantly drawn to her, assuming the peach aroma must be her shampoo.

Humph. She knows my name, which deflates the wind in my rant to a degree. A battle with an unknown is easier than one with a familiar when it comes to this situation. On the ice, it's a different story.

I usually don't get this wound up about management decisions, and the first time I do, I'm at a loss for words, struck by her beauty and calm demeanor. I'm used to girls shouting right back, especially if I'm dating them. I admit I go for the girls who are a bit wild. But you can't fault me for liking those who can party all night with the team.

"Um, I'd like to know why you are pushing Peety to be traded."

I put my palms on her desk and lean forward.

Now, I've resorted to intimidation.

Oddly, throwing my weight around a bit is in my nature. Now, it comes off more like a ploy of intimidation.

"Close the door and have a seat," she replies sternly, sliding her hands under her buttocks to smooth out her long top before taking a seat behind the desk. She closes her laptop to give me her full attention.

Maybe she knows something about hockey. What am I saying, of course she does. You don't get through these doors without knowing your shit. But then again, the GM and the new owner of the team, Greg Anderson, are up here too; at times, their decisions are debatable.

"You shouldn't have that information. Besides, he's not traded. Where did you hear this?" She leans back and picks up a pen to fiddle with, flipping it in and out of the fingers on her right hand.

"I think you have a leak in your office because the press called me. Hell of a way to find out, right before the first round of the playoffs! I'm here because I don't want him traded, period," I demand.

Damn, did I come across as the decider of all things around here? Yeah, I did that.

She remains calm and continues to fidget with the pen, so something must distract her more than my aggressive demands and macho charm.

Even though I'm full of conceit, I have some game. Otherwise, I'd never have a date, and that's never been an issue. Why isn't this working?

Oh God, is there something sticking to my clothing? Did the guys prank me?

I take a beat to regain my composure. This isn't how I imagined this going.

"Well, I can understand where you're coming from, but we can't have players coming up here and protesting everything we do," Callie says, clearly unfettered by my presence.

Now I'm hoping I didn't come across as an ass. I know from experience that angry people are viewed as irrational, and I don't want that. She seems like a nice girl, and she has me second-guessing myself for some reason.

"I know. Sorry about that. I've never been known to fly off the handle with something that doesn't directly affect me. It's just that he means a lot to the team."

I may lose my temper on the ice, but I rarely make a retaliation hit and generally let the enforcer or the player handle it himself. Some of my teammates would prefer if I mixed it up more on the ice but I'm offensive, which means I get the puck in the net.

All I care about is me and my game. The team matters, but I'm the last one to straggle into the locker room because I don't care if I'm late.

"I'm not going to lie about his stats. I'm sure you already know the percentages aren't where we need them."

"I know, it's just that you look at the CORSI numbers, and it doesn't take into account all the other things a player brings to the bench. He's important to the team and the locker room," I try to explain.

"I'm sure he is," she agrees.

Oh no, I don't have a follow-up for that. I wasn't expecting her to agree with me.

I rake my hands through my hair in frustration. "Then why are we even discussing this?"

"It's business." She leans forward, putting her elbow on her desk.

"Business, that's the problem with you people up here. It's all about the bottom line and putting numbers in your stupid little spreadsheets." I'm accusing her of being greedy and heartless.

I can't believe I just insulted her.

"Hold on. I'm not the team's owner or management. I won't argue they can be greedy, but don't stereotype me when you don't know me." Her voice raises as she leans over the desk to stare me down.

"You're right. I don't know you. And you don't know Peety," I counter.

"Well, I don't have to," making air quotes with her fingers, "'know' Peety. All I need to know are the stats showing his performance. That's my job. I suggest you stick to your job, and we'll get along fine."

Typically, I'm neutral and try to avoid the political shit between players and management because each clubhouse has its share of drama. If management wants to move me, and if it's contractually legal, it's a text message and sayonara. That's how quick it is these days.

"I mean, you must be a close friend of his to come up here." She tries to change the subject by putting the pen in a holder on her desk.

When she does this, I notice a framed picture of her in a kayak wearing a nice white bikini, and my cock twitches. She's stacked in all the right places. A picture of a yellow lab wearing a bright pink collar sits beside her. My mind is racing.

So she likes the water. And that must be her dog. I let my eyes drift to her left hand and see no ring. Why am I even looking? There's no way this chick will go out with any guy who just insulted her integrity. I find myself backpedaling to gain a shred of machoism without panicking over the fact that I'm at a loss for how to handle this situation now.

"Um, not the best of friends, but there is so much more to players than stats." She's about to speak, so I put my hand up, palm facing her. "Hear me out. I know you love your numbers. I get it. But how about you spend some time watching Peety and see why he's more important than a number on a piece of paper? Maybe hang out behind us when we're on the bench and get a feel for the team. Y'know?"

She takes in my offer but isn't taking the bait.

"You can have your numbers. I get it. It's your job, and you probably earned a fancy degree to get here, but I'm saying there is more than meets the eye in most situations. I think you'll find it worth your time to revisit it."

She sucks in her cheek a bit. She's thinking. It's not a good look, but I think it's cute. Clearly, she's not pretentious.

She's prettier than I expected for a number cruncher. If she wore glasses, it would only enhance her sexy dark eyes. Her perfectly arched eyebrows are a tad darker—so she's a natural blonde, and her cheeks…. It looks like she spent too much time on a freezing pond, and the wind kissed them, and they turned slightly pink, but still natural looking.

I was hoping to go home, chill out, and play some video games because tomorrow, we have a team meeting on our strategy for the game. But now, she has me thinking about other things, and the boner in my pants could use a seatbelt, so I lean forward a bit in an attempt to hide it.

Damn, I've never been so pissed and turned on at the same time.

6

____

CALLIE

"**O**kay, I'll check Peety out," I concede after the heated exchange, but I'm unsure if it's from the battle of wills over the man on the team or the one in front of me.

Peety. The idea that every guy has a nickname adds another layer of uniqueness to these jocks. They simply added a Y to his first name. Typically, they add a Y to the last name or use some personal characteristic or event, like Tank or Crash.

"Great! We have the game tomorrow, so how about you sit behind us in the stands and just observe the guy at the next game?"

I stand to end the unscheduled meeting. "I can, but I can't promise it will change anything."

What's the harm in going to a game? One game? And one I was planning to go to anyway? Maybe the guy will have an obscene amount of time with the puck, which leads to conversions. Unfortunately, he could play like Gretzky for the entire game but it's not enough to change the overall numbers for the year.

Besides, there's more than just the numbers to take into consideration. It's also about what the team needs to become stronger and unbeatable.

Alexandre extends his hand. "Do we have a deal?"

"Hmm, well, we have a secret deal, and you can't mention this to anyone or what you heard from the press. Those nosy imbeciles ruin everything."

"Okay, I'll be looking for you after the game." He flashes me a rueful smile.

"Oh, I'm not waiting around. I know how y'all will party like rock stars if you win, a shower, a beer or two…" I let my words fall off, insinuating there will be more than dinner and drinks after the locker room closes.

After a solid shake, his hand slides out of mine, and I'm surprised by the softness, considering how many years he's been holding a hockey stick. It felt nice to have a connection with him. Finding someone concerned about a teammate is refreshing, even if he came by the information at an inopportune time.

He has to have huge biceps to send the puck across the blue line, and his wrists can snap a slap shot— even though they aren't legal. Now, they are more akin to what's called a one-timer, a quick release.

Besides, guys who can't send the puck 90 mph or higher don't make it to the pros. I wonder what else he's packing under his Maulers track pants but refuse to lower my eyes to check out 'the goods.' I'm sure he gets that enough from the puck bunnies. What a funny name for hockey groupies.

He turns to leave, and I can't stop myself from checking to see if he has a cute ass to go with the broad back, which shows how small his waist and thighs are—all muscles from weights and skating. I'm envious of how toned he is, and I'm self-conscious for a moment over the fact I don't have the thighs of the twenty-year-old models he hangs out with. I can't help it if they are all built like Greek deities, and their world is comprised of women who have their large bank accounts and are used to the jet set life. I can't fault him for the fact women throw themselves at his feet.

"Y'know, when I first saw you— you seemed preoccupied." He pauses at the door, turning to see my reaction.

My jaw drops a bit. From everything I've heard, he's not a kind, warmhearted jock. He's selfish and conceited. Why is he pretending to care?

"Oh, no, not really." I brush it off like it's nothing, but he's unsatisfied with the answer. I can tell because he's still standing in the doorway waiting for me, to be honest.

"No, I mean, at the door to the suite. When we bumped into each other, which by the way, I'm sorry."

"Oh, that," I cock my head to one side, "nothing really. Just a blast from the past, that's all."

"I'm a good listener. Why don't we do lunch? I can pick you up at noon."

Sarah tells me I need to get out there, and I can't deny he's delightful to look at. A handsome man with an accent— damn those Quebecois accents. What is there to not like about him, except his reputation?

"No, I have work to do." I shrug and turn toward my window, away from him, out of fear I'll accept his invitation. My head says 'no,' but my body screams 'yes.'

Typically, I wouldn't date a player or a person from Canada as their immigration rules and regulations are more of an iron fist situation, but he's hard to resist for a hockey dude, that is.

"Look, you're just going to sit up here and mope around? You're too nice and too pretty not to be smiling. It's gorgeous outside. Summer is fleeting. Meet me." His gentle push catches me off guard.

I never expected for a player to notice me, much less invite me out. It is nice outside, and maybe I'm being too hard on him.

What do I have to lose? It's not like we'll hook up in the middle of the day. I can't miss work. That makes it safe. Eureka!

His persistence might be what I need to get out of my blues and step back into a room with a man.

Against my better judgment, I agree.

"Great, see you at noon." He leaves before I can change my mind.

I walk to my door and glance down the hallway. I have to chuckle because every staff member stops what they are doing to watch him pass by. You'd think he was a movie star the way people ogle him. One guy takes a picture with his cell phone, which is probably against the rules we signed regarding interactions with the players and privacy.

Maybe my ex, Mitch, has taken up enough of my life. I've been moping, or rather hiding, long enough. Either way, I need to stop giving him control over me when it's been over for a long time, and he's never coming back. I need to overcome my fear of making another mistake and find someone to share my life with.

The dating pool consists of boring pilots, guys who want to split the bill on a date, and others who want to get laid. I tried dating after the divorce but felt it was going downhill and stopped before I reached the creepy guy level.

Sarah rushes in, chomping at the bit for information.

"Tell me everything!" She's giddy with excitement and plops into the chair Alexandre just left.

I lean against my desk. "Oh, nothing happened." I wave my hand through the air to dismiss her inquisition.

"I don't believe that for one minute." She smiles at me, and I swear she's holding her breath.

"Ok, you can't say anything, but the press got wind of us trading Peety. Alexandre came up here to vouch for him on the team."

"He's the last player I would expect to do something like that. Did someone spike his protein shake with a conscience?" She snickers.

I get it. He's stuck on himself, late to practice, and had to sit out a game for not being a team player. So yeah, he's a prima donna for sure.

"So, who's the snitch? That shit's confidential." She stands and puts her hand on her hip.

"No idea. Doesn't matter. All that matters is keeping this under wraps so no one on the team finds out until after the playoffs."

It's a good thing Alexandre came to see me. Otherwise, I wouldn't know the press got a whiff of the trade. I return to my desk and sit down before I open my laptop and pretend to look at the screen, hoping Sarah will realize we need to get back to work.

"What happens now?"

"Well, he agreed not to say anything, and we're having lunch."

"Oh, goody." She giggles excitedly and claps her hands like a toddler learning something new.

"It's nothing. He wants me to give Peety another look," I explain.

"Sure he does. I'm sure there's something else he wants you to look at as well." She chuckles. "He's wild, you know. I heard he never uses the name of any girl he's with, calling them all Babe, Mary, or Margaret or something stupid."

"Really?" I find it odd. I change the subject, not wanting to discuss my visitor who has the office buzzing. "But seriously, you're giddy today and normally quiet at work. Who are you?" I tease her as she's been rather naughty lately, especially with all the references to the handsome men around her. "Is there something going on I should know about? Are things at home okay?"

"Oh, God, yes. I mean, my life is filled with three kids, my husband is growing a beer belly since I let him install a kegerator in the house, and I could use more help around the house —you know, the usual stuff. But for now, girl, I'm living vicariously through you."

I'm shocked because I've always looked up to Sarah. She's a few years older and appears to have it all; the husband, the kids, the white picket fence. How can her happily-ever-after compare to my life? Nothing I have going on is newsworthy, but that may have changed.

I say this because, as we talk, co-workers who pass my office door are peering in. I've never been this popular before today.

"I wasn't going to go out with him, but he wouldn't take no for an answer," I volunteer.

I thought she was leaving, but she's waiting for more.

"I can tell he's used to getting his way. He was a bit pushy," I add.

The part about him not using a girl's name is weird. From the photos on the internet, he dates a different swimsuit model every year, but I'm not sure if he's dating one right now.

"Maybe he likes you. Either way, I want all the details," she says as she finally spins on her heels to leave.

Like there is anyone else I can share my personal life with but her. She's been my BFF since I moved back to Maine. Unlike dating, I like getting to know the people who work in this building and know almost everyone here.

I cannot say the same for my high school classmates. Those years were spent feeling like I didn't belong because I'm not the type to join clubs, committees, or teams. Of course, there were other geeks to hang out with, but being so driven, an avid book reader, and into my world, I never did my part to make myself belong.

My high school is only forty minutes down the road, and at the five-year class reunion, it became clear that I had zero interest in attending another one.

Using my keyboard, I begin researching our scouts' program but can't shake Alexandre's visit. Why is he being so nice? He knows I alone don't have the power to stop a trade. However, management will wait until after the playoffs. We have until June, so there's no harm in waiting to see if I missed something.

"The numbers never lie," my dad says. He should know, being

the CFO of the local fish canner. He's proud to call himself a bean counter because numbers are beautiful objects on an Excel spreadsheet when he runs reports.

Sure, things have changed a lot for him, with every year bringing more automation and unemployed workers. Mom works at the University as a secretary to a dean.

Alexandre's attempt to save his teammate is touching. For him to come up here when we all understand and accept that players and management don't mix is an unwritten rule, but it happens to be true. They're playing a sport they love, and we're running a business.

I imagine lunch will be spent watching girls stare at him while I try not to feel guilty for fraternizing with him. I need to keep in mind it's only lunch, and I won't let him influence my recommendations.

He probably wants to try one more time to change my mind, and I'm sure if the guys had their way, no one would ever be traded. If a trade doesn't occur, I'll never hear from him again. So this lunch date might be my 'one-timer' as well.

At least I'm not thinking of Mitch now, and that's progress. I allow him too much space in my head. I should charge him rent, but that's my issue to overcome, not his.

My phone dings. It's a text from Sarah telling me to keep my legs crossed and to have a good time. I glance at the time on my sports watch and realize the morning has passed, and I haven't accomplished anything.

Do girls have sex after a first date that only involves lunch? So much has changed with dating; I don't even know. I've only been with Mitch, so it's weird to think of even kissing someone else. But I can't remember Mitch's kisses, so what harm is there in one working lunch?

7

ALEXANDRE

I can't believe I talked her into saying yes. But hey, I've never had a problem getting what I want from the ladies. Callie hesitated longer than most, but in the end, she caved like so many before her.

I'm still concerned about my teammate's status, but the fact I finagled a date out of Callie lightens the stormy mood I skated in on. I couldn't hold my tongue when I heard the news from the press and came in hot, wanting to unleash my anger on the closest person responsible, even if it wasn't the person responsible for the final decision.

Callie's calm voice and steadfast nature melted the ice from under my skates. I didn't anticipate my rival winning the first round with more finesse than physical might. I'm used to being able to bully and intimidate anyone, but with her . . . I came up empty.

I nod to the cute receptionist sitting outside the GM's office, making sure I'm quiet so I don't disturb him. I hope he's out because I shouldn't be up here.

I don't give a shit about the others most of the time. And right now, I don't recognize myself as I extend my closed fist to give a fan a fist bump before I exit the suite of offices.

I'm glib for no reason, and it's fucking scary.

The possibility of Peety being traded is weighing on me, but I'm confident a lunch is all it will take to get Callie to see things my way. I only need to convince her we need him to win the Cup. A stronger defense, what a joke. Peety can push his weight around; damn the numbers on a spreadsheet. I didn't push her too hard in the office because it's her turf, but lunch will be on neutral ground.

Game on!

I need to create a place for lunch to impress Callie, but it can't be a place screaming money and making her think I'm trying too hard. Something off the beaten path without adoring fans distracting me from my agenda is desirable. I've never cared about anyone's opinion of me, but I don't want her to think I'm a man-whore.

It's fun when a new girl sees my face on a billboard for the first time and recognizes me, but it's hard to know if she's sincere after that.

Dinner dates are often interrupted by my adoring—or not so adoring—fans.

As much as my ego loves the attention, there are days when I want to be me and away from the spotlight. The problem is, I can't remember how it used to be before my name became synonymous with hockey— Juniors and then the NHL.

Maybe I was always a cocky bastard. I do remember I was a skinny puck hog in the Bantam leagues, and a coach set me straight on that, and then our team did better, so I learned the value of sharing the puck, and it forced me to mature.

Typically I wouldn't give a shit about the rest of the team or a girl, but Callie seems different. Quiet, confident, intelligent. She's not the one-and-done type.

She must be driven; otherwise, she wouldn't have her job. I walk to my car as I'm on my phone looking up her bio, and holy shit . . . she has a Ph.D.

I've never dated a brainiac before.

Not that this is a date. I haven't given up on my primary mission to make inroads I might need later.

Where to eat lunch, hmm. A conundrum for sure. I don't want her first impression of me to be a ringside seat to the circus of women throwing themselves at me. There is a place off the beaten path called The Last Kitchen. It's expensive and impossible to get into. No, showing off my spending power is not the way to go. Besides, I don't want it to look like I'm buying her vote.

The Last Kitchen has limited seating, and with it being summer and tourist season, I'm sure it's booked. I'll shelve that idea for another time if there is another time.

As I slide into my brand-new Jaguar, a vision of her occupies my mind. Her long legs and dark eyes are hard to forget. Speaking of hard, I got a boner watching her suck on the end of her pen after she twirled it through her fingers.

Fuck. She's hot and has me acting weird. Like I have the caffeine jitters only I didn't have but two cups all morning. Not enough to have it wreck my body.

I doubt she's ever dated an athlete. Jocks and geeks run in different packs in high school, and it doesn't change much after graduation. Women who love jocks know what they are getting into from the get-go. Callie . . . probably has no idea. Reading people is my secret weapon on the ice, and it works well on opponents. Chicks are my specialty.

I drive along roads with more bends than potholes, even though they are worn from long, rough winters. It occurs to me Callie might have prejudged me. Maybe if she got a glimpse of me not being the reputed asshole, she might take me seriously when I talk hockey with her.

There is another side to me. I can be selfish and arrogant, but I don't broadcast my entire life to the world. The press will always post negative headlines because it makes great clickbait.

Hockey Scoop Magazine outed Wyatt and Emily earlier this year after they paid a greedy condo concierge for insider information.

Fans troll us, and there are tons of re-posts on social media daily. Even our team takes candid shots of us for their purposes. We're fanned out like breadcrumbs for ducks because our faces help sell more jerseys and pricey game day tickets.

Now that we're in the playoffs the tickets will be even more expensive, and ads will be ramped up, resulting in even less privacy. That's when I started to feel like a hooker, pimped out so much, my life was no longer my own, and I had no choice but to play along. If I had a nickel for every time I've made the byline on social media, I'd have another sports car to add to my collection. Just saying.

I drive up the red brick paver driveway leading to my mansion, which I rattle around in, and park outside the three-car garage. I live in one of the newer communities here, explicitly built for my tax bracket. It comes with all the bells and whistles, but I'm not here enough to enjoy it.

We have a community pool, but I prefer the one in my backyard, with a waterfall and hot tub. I can't wrap my mind around public swimming pools. Maybe it comes from growing up in Canada, where frozen ponds and ice rinks outnumber them.

The community pool overlooks the golf course, and the team milks golf season for as long as possible. The earth is frozen, and snow covers the ground, yet we still try to whack the balls. We use golf to keep our swing in the off-season, and it's an opportunity to cut loose. Reporters aren't going to get into our private communities and stalk us out there. Plus, our Tee times are not public information.

Summers are fun and filled with bachelor parties and weddings because there's no time for them during the year. It's also when the water is warm enough to take our jet skis out on the lakes. Some of the guys own boats and enjoy fishing. I'll go with them, but I have no desire to own a boat. Maybe if I lived in Florida, I could use it for over a few months out of the year.

Boys and their toys, we have everything we want and more. Girls aren't the only ones who must keep up with the others in their pack. Men compete, too, and it extends beyond the latest sports car.

I use the keyless double doors to enter my spacious house and hear it automatically close behind me as I walk past one of the two wood-burning fireplaces.

My multi-colored *Saucony* sneakers squeak occasionally as I walk across the tile floor made to look like old wood planks, only its white tile. It's the typical old-world-meets-modern look that's popular now.

The sound of my sneakers echoes off the bare walls. Too bad I'm not an opera singer because my minimalistic interior lends itself to great acoustics.

I walk to the master bedroom and stand in the walk-in closet, debating what to wear. Callie is what I'd consider 'dressed' for work, so I change into a pair of slacks and a nice Polo shirt. It's summer, and I'm allowed to show off my tanned biceps.

The next stop is a master bathroom larger than my first apartment to check my hair and see if I need to shave. Seeing the guys and meeting a girl for lunch requires two different primping protocols.

I pass inspection and have time to kill, so I head to the entertainment room. This is where you'll find the largest TV in the house, a row of theater recliners, a movie screen and projector, and my gaming system. I spend most of my time here when I'm home. As for the formal dining and living room, I haven't even bothered to furnish them. What's the point?

I'm such a hermit. I can't remember the last time I hosted a party. Probably our first season, which is when I came on board, reluctantly, I might add. The Maine Maulers was a new team, and I was told to go. That's how it goes in this business. One text, and you're on the next flight.

The concept of a mother-in-law suite is lost on me when it comes to the rest of the house. I don't know why having one is such a big deal. It sounds funny to me. I call it the second master suite for house guests like my parents, who will come to see me play in the second round. They will live with me for a week or two. Maybe then, the kitchen will get used.

I turn on the TV and check the sports channel for any news about a Mauler's trade. I'm relieved to hear nothing and turn it off. The one thing Callie and I agree on is the fact that any wind of a trade isn't good for the team's morale, so the secret needs to stay in the bag for everyone's sake.

8

CALLIE

Nowadays, it's rare to see a man wearing a suit unless you're at a wedding or a funeral. Many offices no longer require business attire unless it's a publicized event. Those of us who live in Maine tend to wear more because most of the year, it's cold.

I casually make my way to Sarah's desk for some friendly chit-chat and reinforcement. I feel like a traitor for even agreeing to meet Alexandre. I'm nervous I'll have either nothing to say or the opposite—I'll talk too much and make a fool of myself.

The fact I'm leaving the building for lunch is normally enough to cause my cubicle coworkers to pop up like meerkats, but today, no one seems to notice.

Instead, everyone is preoccupied with calling their friends to give a play-by-play describing their chance encounter with Alexandre. With all the commotion, you'd think they spotted Bigfoot.

It's our routine to get together for lunch, and Sarah raises her eyebrows as I plop into a chair across from her. Her cat-like grin conveys her approval of my upcoming secret meeting with the man of the hour, the one the office is still abuzz about.

All this sneaking around has me feeling like my dog Lucy,

whose idea of fun is to see if she can get scraps out of the trash can as soon as I turn my back. She is more accomplished at surfing the kitchen counters for food than I am at surfing the internet for shoe bargains. She even ate my TV remote. Thankfully it was replaced by an employee at the cable company who has a dog just like her at home. He was gracious enough to not charge me for it.

"So, hot date, huh?"

"Ha, I'm sure there's only one thing on Alexandre's mind. Peety."

"I wouldn't be so sure about that." She leans back in her chair, a smug look on her face.

"I'm not on any menu for a beefy guy like him. I've seen the girls he goes out with, all swimsuit and lingerie models."

"Like I said, no one else is rushing up here to save Peety."

A pang of regret hits me. I won't be sharing lunch with her in the break room today. We normally split a sandwich from home and a bag of chips from the vending machine. Eating out is expensive, and it's a pain to drive around, not to mention the long walk through the parking lot in heels. I forgot my lunch today, so this is perfect.

"I know. His buddy might be a favorite in the locker room, but I have a job to do. Plus, lunch outside the office sounds good for a change."

"Wish I had you bugged so I could hear you two and know how lunch is going. You should have seen his jaw drop when you entered your office."

"I doubt that."

Maybe he was surprised to see a woman doing what he expected was a man's job. He seems to think Peety's fate is up to me alone, but there's more to it. Ultimately, I'm only the messenger, and the final decision is above my pay grade.

"Yeah, well, we'll see."

Sarah gets up to head toward the break room, "Have fun and try not to bore him with talk about how you arrive at compiling data."

She gives me a stern look, "No shop talk on anything he doesn't bring up first."

"Oh, right." Of course, she is an expert in dating. She's the one with the family life, not me. I trust her judgment. "Should I break out a cheerleader sweater instead? This is not 1950, I have a mind, and it's okay to show it."

"Yes, but ease him into it, don't blurt out the history of numbers. You tend to speak a mile a minute, and he hasn't been conditioned for that." She pauses. "I'm sure he's conditioned for more important things that will bring you more satisfaction if you give it a chance." She flashes a coy smile my way.

Ouch. I raise eyebrows as if to say, 'Really?'

"You can be a bit intense," she explains. "You know I love you just the way you are. I'm just saying not all jocks are loved for their IQ. If you catch my drift."

This gives me one more reason to hide behind my books, numbers, and dog. In fact, Lucy has a more appealing personality, and it dawns on me to take her on dates. Dogs are chick bait for guys, maybe it would work for me, too.

I'm an achiever. I'm uncontrollable when it comes to achieving. I'm the go-to girl. I do more in one day than most mortals accomplish in five. I may not understand men, but I do know myself. And believe me when I say my personality can be a blessing and a curse.

"Hey, I'm going out with a guy, aren't I? How many changes do you expect in one day?"

"As many as I think you need," she sighs, "trust me, this is a step in the right direction."

"Good to know." How can I take offense when she has my best interest at heart?

I attend our staff meeting and the powers that be want to make a trade. I'm the one who needs to find a suitable player who will boost our team's defense and find a guy that's a bit of a bargain to not push us over our salary cap.

Great, just what I needed, more stress. I might as well start taking medication for heartburn now with how my day is shaping up.

I return to my desk and stare at the blank computer screen. I desperately attempt to accomplish something, I check the calendar on my phone. According to my notes, I'm supposed to be compiling the stats on some of the rookies we are looking at for the draft in June.

I log into the scouts' database to log their reports and fill in numbers. My office phone rings just as I'm fully immersed in the facts and figures.

"Hello, Callie Dobek."

"I'm out front. If you're not here in five minutes, you turn into a pumpkin." Alexandre's playfulness scores a six on the cuteness scale.

"I'm no princess," is the only retort I can think of. I'm surprised he hasn't already figured out I'm no princess. I'm nerdy and boring. A job dealing with numbers all day should have been his first clue.

"That's where you're wrong," his tongue-in-cheek response catches me off guard, and I stifle a chuckle, but at the same time, his compliment is unexpected and makes me smile.

He's probably not coming to get me because of all the suits up here. By that, I mean management. They make all the guys uncomfortable. Jocks and suits resemble suede boots in the snow—a hot mess of ugliness.

I'm sure he wants to avoid more commotion in the office. From what I've seen online, he's not the type to avoid the spotlight when the cameras are on.

I confess I looked up his social media accounts, and every woman on his arm looks like a model with tits the size of my head and waist the size of my wrist.

I grab my purse and pass by the break room to give Sarah a nervous half-smile. "See ya."

"Remember, have fun," are her parting words.

I wonder how does one have fun with lunch?

When she says fun, does she mean sex? Am I missing something? How does one have fun with what's mostly hand-holding? Not to mention the fact that we're strangers and probably have nothing in common.

I have half a mind to turn around, intimidated by the girls on his Instagram. My stomach does a flip flop, and my heart is racing as I wait for the elevator, and I override my initial gut feeling to run back to my office.

My sense of decency prevails, of course, as I'm dependable and courteous, so I pop out of the building and enter the parking lot.

Sure as shit, Alexandre is waiting, leaning against the passenger side of his Jag, arms crossed and a big grin on his face.

My heart melts. It's like a scene in a movie as he steps aside and opens the door for me.

I notice he's changed into a fresh shirt and slacks. He looks sharp. I'm surprised he's punctual because he has a habit of being late to practice.

Interesting.

"Hey," he greets me, taking off his designer sunglasses with the blue reflective coating, making him look like the multi-millionaire he is. What can I say? He wears it well. I can't challenge perfection when it comes to the man's genetics for looks, fashion, and, apparently—charm.

"Hi," I say, staring into eyes the color of the ocean while I try to lower myself into the seat gracefully. I'm too low to the ground because I feel like I'm in a go-cart. But, judging from the new car smell and luxurious interior, this is no wood box with wheels.

I wonder how many of his girlfriends have sat in this same seat. At 5'7 they must know how to fold themselves like an origami bird to fit. It's doable because Alexandre is taller than me, as in- he's over six feet tall.

He shuts my door before he walks around the front of the car, looking very buff. His clothes fit perfectly, snug to accentuate his tight ass and biceps.

I groan. I'm a sucker for a tight ass.

"I hope you're not expecting a fancy lunch," he says, sliding into the driver's seat.

"No problem." I click the seatbelt in place. "Driving to lunch in this car is fancy by all means."

His chuckle relieves my anxiety after being on my first date in over a year. Maybe I misjudged him, and he really isn't stuck on himself as much as rumor has it. With any rumor, there is a seed of truth, and his seed was planted by trainers and coaches who talk to management; therefore, I consider it to be reliant.

Anyone who follows hockey knows Alexandre's name is synonymous with playboy bachelor, along with a side of arrogance. I tend to prejudge all the players as having egos bigger than their dicks, so I would not be surprised if he's just another jock with too much testosterone.

There are exceptions to every rule. And I love the videos on social media of the guys who have outrageously expensive summer weddings at a swanky venue with a six-tiered cake and the entire team around them.

Within a year or two, they post pictures of their adorable newborns in the Stanley Cup. When I see stuff like that, it reminds me I haven't found the right guy yet, and I need one of those to start a family.

I secretly yearn for kids and am envious of Sarah's home life, just like she lives vicariously through me. Could it be a touch of the 'grass is always greener?'

"So, where are we going?"

"Patience, Padawan." He puts the car in gear and turns to give me a charming smile.

I understand first-hand how his perfect looks and deep voice can get a woman's panties to slide off without lifting a finger.

His *Star Wars* reference is not lost on me. I'm digging his sense of humor.

"It's not too far from here," he volunteers. "Do you like music?"

"Um, yeah, but not rap. I don't understand it, and I hate classical."

"I do, too. Nothing like music from the 90s, and you can't go wrong with rock."

From a laptop-sized screen on the dash, he selects a music channel that streams hits from the 80s and runs right up to today's music.

I'm glad he keeps the volume low because I find it difficult to talk over loud music, preferring to only play music when I'm alone in the car.

Sitting this close, I detect the scent of spicy vetiver grass and cedar wood. It reminds me of a freshly sharpened number two pencil, and it's a nice change from riding alone everywhere I go and no man in sight.

I love the outdoors and applaud a man who can wear strong colognes and yet not overpower my nose or fire up my allergies.

"So, busy day or what?"

"Nope." I omit the fact I stared at a blank computer screen, unable to concentrate.

Shit, shit, shit.

Do all jocks have this mesmerizing power over females? Is it why women flock to these guys like ducks looking for handouts of left-over bread?

I still haven't figured out why I'm here, in his car, on my way to lunch. Then again, I haven't had a date in seven months, and it will keep Sarah from nagging me for a week or two.

Surely this is a one-time deal so he can solidify his teammate's safety. I'd be a fool to expect anything less. I'm very analytical. I'm not deviating from my skillsets to make allowances for the dreamy man who is making time to spend time with me when I'm sure he has better things to do.

Like calling his agent for a commercial promoting a new drink made with flavored vodka.

I expect to get hit with more questions about the trade because he gave up way too fast this morning. At this juncture, I might be disappointed if he doesn't put up a fight. It would mean my analytics indicator is askew.

And right now, he has me at a loss as we are headed to a mysterious place for lunch, and I'm trusting him to make these decisions without any input.

9

———

ALEXANDRE

Callie looks lovely sitting in my car with the early afternoon sunlight, her blonde hair kissed by the sun.

"So, where are we going?"

She has her guard up with me, and why not… considering I'm more the black sheep of hockey than the favorite son.

"We're going to a place you'd least expect," I tease and catch her wringing her hands in her lap. Maybe she's not trusting of men, and I should reassure her I'm not a serial killer.

"Really?"

"Don't worry. We won't be alone," I promise her.

I can tell the wheels in her head are spinning as she tries to figure out where we're headed. I focus on the curvy road ahead and pass over a short bridge covering one of the many natural creeks indicative of Maine. Most towns and creeks are Indian names, but I'll be damned if I can pronounce any of them.

She appears anxious, and I can't help but enjoy it just a bit. The fact I can drive her nuts by keeping her in the dark is cute.

As I said, I'm not an angel.

Every accountant I've ever met loves order and tends to be meticulous. I am with a female accountant, and she's a bit uptight.

I can come up with a dozen things I can do to help her overcome her stiffness, but I keep it to myself.

"Is it close?" She's not worried about me kidnapping her, and I shouldn't be teasing her so much, but I find it amuses me.

"Sure is." I use my left hand to turn the wheel with my palm and my right hand to shift as I pull up in front of an ice rink in a neighboring community.

"This is lunch?" Her voice proves it's a preposterous idea, but I've sparked her interest as she leans forward to get a better look at the building.

I'm stoked. I have her by the way she does a double take on the hand-painted sign and mouths the words Kennebunk Arena.

"It's a hockey rink," she exclaims.

"Yep," I say, turning off the car. "Come, you'll like it."

Our eyes lock, and a slight smile graces her perfect heart-shaped lips, lips as sweet as a plump juicy strawberry at the end of summer.

Happiness, Or is that relief washing over her face?

I wonder if she skates.

We walk through the doors and into a near-empty arena, enjoying the blast of cold air. There aren't many people here this time of day, but we see some kids taking private lessons on one of the rinks. All three rinks are large enough for regulation games, and there's a third rink where the owner holds the ECHL games and concerts, so it has stadium seating.

"Wait, this is where the Kennebunk Megalodons play, isn't it?"

"Yes, it is."

See, this woman knows her shit about hockey.

"Lunch is this way." I tilt my head toward the larger arena and the food venue.

"Hot dogs?" she inquires as we approach a concession stand selling handheld food and bottled drinks.

"We could, but I thought you'd prefer the restaurant upstairs."

"Oh," her posture perks up, "no problem. I've never been here."

"Great, we can watch the kids on the rink from upstairs. It's a sports bar with TVs, but the food is so much better. Most people don't know there's a great chef here."

"Of course there is. Like you would eat just anywhere?" she teases me.

"Hey, we can turn around, and I'll eat a hot dog with you, even splurge on some French fires covered in melted nacho cheese."

"Really?"

"I'm just going with the flow, Callie." I keep walking just the same.

She chuckles, but I'm not sure why she finds this funny.

I take her by the hand to guide her in the right direction around a corner. She doesn't pull away, and her touch sends warmth up my arm, just like a brandy would warm my lungs on a winter day snowmobiling in freezing temperatures. I like how soft her hand is, and the warmth is spreading to other areas of my body.

Fuck.

My goddamn boner is eliciting a party in my pants, and it's increasingly harder to ignore. I fake my walk, hoping she doesn't notice.

Instead, she's watching the kids on the bench we pass around the nearby elevator as they put their skates on while mothers entertain their other kids and wait for lessons to end.

I press the button on the elevator. She seems fine with her hand in mine as I let her step in first.

The doors open on the second floor, and we step into a waiting area outside the restaurant decorated in a nautical theme with lots of driftwood, fishing nets, and lobster traps.

"I hope you like seafood. Their New England Clam Chowder is very good. It's warm outside, so you might want a cold soup."

Her quizzical look gives me pause. "Or no soup. Maybe you don't like soup."

I tilt my head and wait for her to say something, but she giggles.

Not much, but I heard it, and I think she might be having a good time.

"I will go on the record and state I don't have any issues with soup."

"Good, I was worried for a minute," I tease.

"Really?"

Inside the restaurant, the hostess approaches, and I put up two fingers and wait to be seated.

"Nope." My deadpan delivery brings out a real chuckle, and I'm glad she's seeing a different side to me, one I normally only share with the guys, and it's not often. I tend to keep to myself.

What the hell is happening to me?

Fuck me; I said her name. Now I'm trying to make her smile.

"Besides, we all know New England Clam Chowder is better than Manhattan chowdah," and she says it the way a New Yorker would.

"I beg to differ, Manhattan chowdah," I make sure to annunciate it even more, "is better."

"You're not serious," she takes the bait.

"Why sure." We follow the hostess. "Isn't it better?"

"Oh, no, who wants clear broth with a tomato base and vegetables? I mean, come on. We're Maniacs. We grow potatoes, and the cream in it is to die for. The thick creamy goodness mixed with the clams makes me eat it non-stop."

"Ah, gotcha. I love New England Clam Chowder."

She pauses, and a stunned look covers her brow. "You're putting me on?"

"Yeah, I mean, what real Mainer would like red chowder?"

"Exactly." She lets out a slight snicker in relief.

The hostess leads us to a booth, and I let go of her hand so she can scoot in.

We take the menus, and the hostess leaves.

"I have a confession, you looked like you were having a rough morning when we met, so I wanted to cheer you up and make you laugh."

"Well, thanks, that's sweet," she demurely replies.

I notice her toned arms are tanned and wonder what else she likes to do besides kayaking.

The waitress brings us menus and water and says she'll be right back.

"Is there anything I can do? You seemed upset."

"Oh, yeah, it wasn't anything, really. My ex."

"Ex as in boyfriend . . .?"

"Husband."

"Oh. Sorry about that."

The waitress returns for our order, and after conferring with Callie, we decide on lobster rolls and iced teas.

Seeing as how we're in Maine and all.

"Yeah, I should be over it. It's been two years. I mean, like. . ." She shakes her head, knowing it's old news.

"That's a long time."

"Yes, it is. I'm just not one to take marriage lightly, and I was busy with my classes, and I guess he got lonely."

"Another woman?"

"Yep. He called me just before you showed up. He wants the leather jacket I bought him, and I hate to admit it, but I saved it after the divorce. I don't know why, and I'm not proud of it." She shrugs and looks down at her hands resting on the table.

She's a breath of fresh air, a genuine person who's been hurt, and I can't stop myself from sympathizing with her.

"It's his loss."

"I know, it's easy to say, much harder to feel that way every day, day in and out. The anger, y'know?"

"I get it. Unfortunately, I've never been married, so saying I understand would be an exaggeration."

"Right. I knew that."

"You did, did you?" I can't keep the satisfaction out of my voice, knowing she must have looked me up. This means she has to be interested in me.

She blushes like she's sixteen and her parents just embarrassed her in front of her first boyfriend. I'm in awe of such sweetness when I normally surround myself with superficial women who are not the blushing type.

"I confess, I had to look you up." She flips her hands outwards and palms up. It's as if she's acknowledging she was caught.

"So you are honest, except when it comes to leather jackets?"

"Pretty much." She nods.

"I get that. I do. Women often leave with something of mine. Boxers, toothbrushes. It's weird sometimes."

"That's really weird." Her smile melts me as my heart grows bigger.

What the hell is going on? I'm walking around with boners, warm tingly feelings running through my body when we touch, and I'm enjoying myself.

She gazes at the rink below, watching the little tykes on skates, pointing and making comments, enjoying the cuteness of them falling down and getting back up.

"I take it you like kids."

"Um, yeah. That's what hurt so bad today. My ex is having a baby, and here I am, older, and not much on the horizon but my career."

"Now that I can identify with." I grin as I sip my tea, and our gazes cross like lightsaber wands.

The food arrives, and I discover she likes dipping her fries in mayo, a European way of eating them. In Belgium, it's called 'treats' and sold on the sidewalks out of food trucks today or little stands.

"Have you traveled?"

"Oh, no. I want to. Boy, do I want to, but nope. All work and no play— you know how it goes."

"Yeah, I do." I wait for Callie to take a bite out of her sandwich before I do the same.

"Boy," she dabs her lips, lips I long to kiss, with a paper napkin, "this lobster is amazing. Good call."

"Hey, I know things." I make it like I'm brushing my shoulder with the back of my fingers like I'm an expert at everything before I take another bite.

She notices, and instead of calling me out on my bullshit, she rewards me with yet another smile. I can't help but feel I made someone's day better today; for the time being, I've forgotten about my own agenda.

10

——————

CALLIE

So Alexandre the Arrogant appears to have a soft side but I'm not getting sucked in. Once was enough. No way am I going through all the pain of loving a man who no longer loves me.

Finding out Mitch had a girlfriend hit me like a shot of whiskey, reeking of lighter fluid, and it burned from my lips to my stomach. When he left, he might as well have run over my heart and soul with a cement truck.

Men may woo me, but how can I trust any of them? Certainly not a man like Alexandre. Sure, he's observant, sharp, and dedicated, but he may as well wear a sign around his neck that reads, "Don't touch; if you do, you'll get burned."

Knowing this, will it be enough to quell the butterflies in my stomach when I hear his voice over the phone? Or enough to say no if he tries to make a move?

He's dangerous. He has money to do what he wants when he wants. Men like him get used to having everything their way, and it's tough for an independent woman like me to find a compromise. He will be set in his ways, and I doubt he's changing soon.

From social media, I gather he's having a great time as a bachelor and loves his life the way it is. I don't know why I agreed to see him. I thought he wanted to talk about Peety, but surprisingly he wants to talk about me.

"Why am I even sharing this with you?" I ask point blank, because this conversation is normally reserved for Sarah and girl's night out.

"Maybe you feel comfortable. I hate leaving things to chance as well. It could be why I'm still single. I like facts and details. When I practice with the puck, I want to know where I'm shooting and where it will hit the net. I love to study the complexities of how it can bounce and spin. I know it's insane to overthink it, but I'm crazy that way."

His eyes suddenly cloud over as if he's had a bad flashback or discovered something profound about himself.

"So what about you?" he asks, finishing his sandwich and starting on his fries. He loves ketchup, and I watch him lap it like a swim team.

"We've covered loves and losses. When do you want to talk about Peety?"

"Oh." He wipes his hands on a napkin. "Peety will be fine wherever he goes. I don't want it to affect our chance at the Cup. Don't get me wrong; it would crush him. It's never easy to say goodbye unless we hate the player or the coach. But Peety, he's the heart and soul of the locker room. You'll see for yourself when you're at the game tomorrow. No?" His incredible scent wafts across the table, and I squirm in my seat.

"For sure." However, I have no idea how this just tumbled out of my mouth without a thought.

Is he always this smooth? Like when he held my hand, it felt so natural to have his fingers interlaced with mine. My heart thumped like a racehorse, and I prayed my hand wouldn't start sweating before we reached the booth.

Uncomfortable with the intimacy, I stare out the window,

watching the kids learn how to skate. They're all so cute, tiny, and determined to have fun and learn at the same time. I should learn to do the same and lighten up.

"There might be another hockey star down there right now," I mumble.

"True, especially if their birthday is in January or February; they have a jump start on the kids born later in the year, thus more time on the ice when they start playing."

"Are you bullshitting me?"

"No, it's actually a fact." He pays the check with a hundred-dollar bill, and we get up to leave.

Hmm, he just left a huge tip to the waitress, and sure enough, she calls out a thank you, and she uses his name as we leave.

"You must come here often."

"Well. . ."

"Oh, no, don't tell me you own this place." Did I miss that detail when I was trolling his online profile earlier?

"Oh, no. No time. Too much commitment." We walk off the elevator on the ground floor, and I see a huge poster for youth hockey sign-ups to attend Alexandre Holloway's hockey camp.

I stop, wrapping my mind around the obvious. Is Alexandre, the wild bachelor, lending his name to a youth summer camp? This can't be true.

"You? Really?" I ask, pointing at the sign.

"Oh, yeah." A hint of embarrassment is on his chiseled face. Charitable and modest, I'm intrigued.

I don't think too many people get to see this side of him. How come this isn't splashed everywhere like his trysts?

"I come and do a few lessons with the kids every summer. We have great coaches working with the kids. We even give out a few scholarships because the camp is expensive. Overhead, not me." It's apparent he wants me to know, and he's not doing it for notoriety.

I believed the media, and maybe they have him all wrong. I

thought he was more of the *Grinch that Stole Christmas*. Is it possible his heart is growing?

It seems important to him that I know this. Yet–I can't figure out his angle. What does he have to gain?

He must be reading my mind, adding, "I don't broadcast it because I don't want to overshadow the kids here. I do some quiet fundraising with the guys. I have help."

"That's nice." It's all I can think of as a reply when he opens my car door.

I no longer see him as the ass the media makes him out to be. But anyone can put up a façade and keep it going for a long time, experience has taught me that life lesson.

"Well, thanks for lunch. I have to say it wasn't what I thought it would be."

"You mean you thought it would be over the top or I'd be a jerk?"

"Maybe a bit of both, as long as we're being honest."

"I'm all for honesty." With that, he pulls out of the parking lot, and we make small talk on the ride back to work.

I suck at being superficial, so I fall back on what I know best, work. I tell him about the degrees I obtained and was surprised to learn he was pre-law before he dropped out to play hockey.

I told him I loved watching hockey games with my dad as a kid but never thought I'd be good enough to play on a team. This job is the closest I can get to the game and get paid well at the same time.

The rink where we had lunch was out of town so by the time, he dropped me off, I was running late. I approach Sarah's desk, hoping to slip by, but it's useless. She's got a sixth sense, like Kathy Bates in a thriller movie, and she's lying in wait for me.

"So, how was it?"

She takes one look at my face. "You talked about numbers, didn't you?" she jumps up from her chair to follow me.

"A little, at the end," I pause, "but not much now that you mention it. He kept me distracted, I guess."

"That's a plus. So what's he like?"

"I'm surprised. He's nice as far as I can tell."

"Well don't say that to Cindi Lamper, the up-and-coming Toronto model he recently broke up with. I guess she hit her expiration date six months in."

"I didn't realize they were an item. I saw headlines, but I don't pay much attention to gossip. Now, when it comes to player engagements and weddings I wanna hear all about it."

It's the romantic in me. I'm a sucker for a happy endings.

"Oh yes, their weddings—off the hook amazing." She draws it out like a New Yorker, but she's a local girl like me, and I chuckle.

"Oh, you're getting your sense of humor back," I tease.

"Hmm, maybe, you are going to the game with me tomorrow, aren't you?"

"Sure, as long as you pay for those pricey seats," she replies. Her grin gives away her excitement.

"I gotcha covered, girl," I reply, turning on the back of my heels to return to my office.

Now the office feels quiet, and I miss the sounds of the kids in the arena. I kind of miss Alexandre, too.

I tap away at my keyboard, determined to look up this Cindi chick.

Hmm, tall, gorgeous, everything I imagined and more. She's Canadian, which is a plus since he's from there.

The building is buzzing with the fanfare and sellout crowd expected for the Boston Sharks game tomorrow. Shark fans will be coming up from Boston because the tickets to their stadium are way more expensive and limited. Even during a bad year, they sell out every game because hockey is huge in the north, and Bostonians and New Englanders love their sports teams and pay top dollar to see them live.

My phone rings. It's the ticket office.

"Hey, Callie. I'm calling to let you know Mr. Holloway left you two tickets to the game tomorrow night, front and center. Those are the best seats in the house."

"Oh, well, thanks."

It seems like this bad boy is making good on promises even before he knows his teammate's fate. The players understand their careers are secondary to management's objectives, and nothing in life is guaranteed, not even for them.

I stare at the stack of reports on my desk and wonder if I'm right about my commitment to the numbers I finesse. I doubted myself after my breakup. Mitch and I looked great on paper but we didn't work out. Who's to say one player can make that much of a difference on or off the team? Again, maybe I've wasted my time on this career if it turns out my results aren't valid.

True, there is little room for human objectivity and the intangible worth a player brings to the team. Now, Alexandre has me rethinking the entire process, and it's the last thing I want to address.

Maybe I'm the one who is set in their ways. Have I become so uptight I can't see another person's view unless it can be quantified into an Excel spreadsheet?

Even though I wouldn't say I like uncertainty, I stop listening to the voices in my head. For now, I hope the team wins their first game.

11

ALEXANDRE

I drop Callie off at the arena. I head home, but I'm full of energy. I need to keep busy. This is not the time for pre-game jitters. Her cute smile drives me crazy, and her story really touched me. This is the first time I've ever listened to how a woman struggles emotionally after her man cheats.

I see the guy's side of it since I've hung out with a team forever, and there is usually some drama over women. Some of the guys play their part as well.

Callie and I have similar personalities, and it's a relief to talk without the intrusive fans and media attention who scrutinize our every move. She's not active on social media, and she's not an influencer like the younger girls I normally date therefore, she's not constantly glued to her phone.

Callie is clearly a woman who has adulted and also has a sense of purpose of where she's going in life. I might not know all the details, but she's too put together to be unorganized.

Personally, most younger women don't have a clue what they want out of life. Their idea of adversity is to be locked out of their social media account for a day or lose a fake nail in a pool party—things I don't give a shit about.

Callie is jaded, but I've dated jaded women before. Most men break up with women who have trust issues with men and move on, leaving the women wondering if they are pretty enough and smart enough. I get it. It can take its toll on the most confident of women.

I hang out in the entertainment room playing virtual golf to get my mind off Callie. But I can't forget how her eyes lit up at lunch as she watched the tykes skate. Her reaction was priceless, an actual Hallmark moment if I ever witnessed one, and I wish she could see herself the way I see her.

I'm confident I hit the first date out of the park. Should I even consider it a date? She's just a new contact, one of many, and she needed to be cheered up. I have no clue what possessed me to ask her out, but she handled my outburst well, and I figured I owed her.

I've known her for two minutes, but I can appreciate how hard she worked to be where she is today, and we have that in common. Only, I'm making millions, and my world is filled with contractual obligations, high finances, and a lifestyle many envy. Her daily grind is crunching numbers and appeasing what management dictates to strengthen our team.

I understand now how her ex's surprise phone call wrecked her day. Why did he call to bother her about a stupid jacket? He should have just bought a new one. Or did he call because he's fishing for something?

I have more important things to do than determine people's motives when they have nothing to do with me. My job is to make plays that win games.

The breakup with my last girlfriend, Cindi, recently went viral, even though it's been over for a few months. The press doesn't need to get the facts right to time stamp it into a vault of meaningless information, the stuff I refer to as my life. The truth is relationships would be easier without so many people meddling.

Why does everyone have to have an opinion? They post shit on social media, like assuming a player has a coke habit when our noses are runny when we get off the ice. Whose nose doesn't run in cold weather?

My opinion is the only one that matters. I know this, and I'm cocky, but I have days where I take my beatings, and it's not all on the ice. I try to remain positive, but haters want to hate. Nothing I can do about that, so I try to skirt the negativity.

Do I get a bad rap for not having a girlfriend who lasts for more than a year? Sure, all the time, the haters blame me and say it's because I'm a prick.

All they know is that I constantly and consistently remain a bachelor no matter how attractive the girl. There are a couple of reasons why. For one, I don't want a long-distance relationship with both of us traveling for our careers. And two, I have no intentions of getting married.

That's also why I don't use their real names. Instead, I use Babe, Honey, Mary, or Maria. To avoid falling in love, Julia Roberts didn't kiss on the lips. I don't say my girlfriend's name. However, I realized at lunch I slipped up.

Most of the girls I've dated weren't looking for marriage either. They all start off agreeing to the terms, but some fall in love. When I'm unable to return it, I'm sure it hurts. Some get vindictive, some move on, and the last blasted me on social media.

When she talked about her ex-husband, the hurt look on Callie's face reminded me of Cindi's face the last time I saw her. I probably wouldn't have recognized it if not for my break-up months ago.

These girls have been on this circuit for years, moving up the rungs of their careers just like me. Some adore the limelight, and others don't. It's not for everyone.

I had a girl break it off because she wanted a life outside of the public's invasive eye. Believe it or not, the idea of another vacation on a jet seems more taxing than enjoyable to some. I live in the fast lane, and there are casualties along the way. I can't say I'm perfect.

I've got my quirks. It's gonna take one hell of a woman to tame my wild ass.

But with Callie, I'm horny as hell, and I'm open to putting myself back on the market. Until she gives me an indication she's interested, I'm okay hanging with the guys. Knowing about the potential trade is difficult when I can't talk to any of them about it. Keeping this huge secret from my friend and the team is a headache.

Even though I stay at arm's length, the guys are all my brothers. However, I am vested in Peety because he helps keep us mentally where we need to be before a game, brings out the best in all of us, and pushes us to be where we are today.

I often overthink the game and run scenarios through my mind as I dress. I can talk myself down, but it helps when my teammate entertains us with his witty banter and bad jokes. Peety isn't afraid to go as far as he needs to elicit a response from us.

I decide I'm better off keeping my promise to Callie, which means I might have to tell a white lie to my buddy. I wouldn't want to know about this before the biggest game in my life. And I rationalize there is always the probability that even if they want to trade him, he might not be part of the final deal.

Like I say, nothing good will come from the team getting worked up over this, especially on the eve of our first playoff round. With this in mind, I take one for the team and say nothing.

It's not like me to care so much, and he's a big boy. Moving from team to team is the norm in our world. Few players spend their entire career with one team, and I've been moved once already. It's a constant turnover in pursuit of the dream team every owner, GM, and coach wants.

We all want to win, but, for the athletes, it comes at a cost. Many of us still stay in touch with our old teammates. Even if we fall out of touch, there is usually an extra pat on the back when we knock into each other during a rivalry game.

I haven't heard from Callie, and it's to be expected. We didn't get chummy enough for me to ask for her phone number, and the last thing I want to do is make her uncomfortable when she might not be ready to date.

Wait, did I think about dating her?

Fuck me.

THE ENERGY in the arena is contagious as the equipment manager buzzes around making sure we have everything we need. Trainers run around, reminding us to stretch and warm up.

The digital clock on the wall says we have thirty minutes until game time.

"What were you up to yesterday?" Wyatt sits beside me, putting on his skates.

"Funny thing happened. I met a girl."

He chuckles. "Tell me something I don't know."

"Her name is Callie."

Wyatt freezes.

Victor stops wrapping his stick with tape because the bomb I just dropped makes him mess up the perfectly symmetrical lines he's making on the blade. It's his ritual before a game, and now he'll have to redo it. His look of annoyance changes to disbelief as his jaw drops an inch, and he asks, "Did I hear you say Callie?"

"Yeah, you know her or something?" My voice raised an octave. Oh, God, I hope he didn't date her.

I pray to God he doesn't, or I will have to make up an excuse not to blow her cover.

All the guys stop what they are doing to listen.

"You just said your girl's name." Peety looks at me like I'm bonkers.

Maybe I am.

Fuck, did I just do that? How many years have I called the girls anything but their given names?

The habit that has given me a reputation over the years just went down in flames. The façade is over.

"It's not her real name," I try to cover for my slip, but the guys all start to dance around with 'oohs' and 'aahs'.

Then they rush in for more details, details they're not getting tonight.

I've said enough.

"It is her real name," Peety says, slapping my back. "You are a goner, man. Next one getting married. I called it." He points his first two fingers like he's predicting the winning lottery numbers in advance.

"No, no, and hell no." Me? Married?

Make that *fuck no*.

It's laughable, but I'm the only one in the room in a panic as the music is cranked up again, and the guys return to their game day routine.

"I'm not living this one down, am I?"

"Not a chance," Wyatt chuckles. "Callie, hmm, wasn't that a horror movie before my time?"

"The movie was *Carrie,* and it's nothing. Really, I just fucking slipped up. Must be the excitement of the playoffs."

"Hey, Zander, don't let it mess with your head." Wyatt finishes his skates and stands to put his chest protector over his bare and toned chest.

Most of us compare ourselves to each other. We're known to be vain, and I can't deny it's true.

"Sure." I hand him his jersey.

I can tell Wyatt's just giving me lip service.

And why did I slip up and say her name? She's too smart to date me, especially after her train wreck of a marriage. She needs to find someone safe, or she'll get hurt again.

Callie is proud, determined, and pursuing her dreams. She's a tough cookie with some baggage and her only setback has been marriage. I doubt she wants to go down that road again. And it's a cold day in the Sahara when I agree to get hitched.

The way I see it, the pressures of the road, the late-night phone calls when we're stuck in an airport or have to go to another city and can't make it home disappoints the family. It's tough, and you add a few kids to that, and the stress goes up, as does the divorce rate.

We make the big bucks, but everyone would be doing it if it were that easy.

Normally, all I look for in a woman is one who's good-looking and nice. But after today, I have a new appreciation for women who make order out of chaos.

Maybe I'm her next work in progress. If she can find the good in a pile of numbers, perhaps she can find a shred of decency in me; maybe there is enough to make me an acceptable suitor.

Coach comes in, and the music is turned off. He gives his pep talk and leaves.

Wyatt and I take shots of Red Bull and coffee as part of our pre-game good-luck ritual. Five minutes later, I snap on my helmet, grab my stick near the exit and follow the guys into the hallway. The past few years have been a struggle to get here, but our day is here at last.

The music vibrates, and fans cheer as the announcer kicks off the evening. The fog from the dry ice machine fills the rink, and we rush out of the tunnel.

My skates hit the ice.

We make a lap inside our zone and take warm-up shots on our goalie. I hang by the boards and stretch my legs beside Kal, our Alternate Captain.

"Ready for this, Bagel?"

"Sure thing, Zaney," he quips.

Let's face it, there aren't many Jewish guys who play hockey. Kal's family probably expected him to be an accountant or stockbroker because he has a financial planning degree. He's a jock with a kickass head for numbers and the uncanny ability to always knows where the puck is. He's like an eagle on the ice. His ice sight and intuition are so instinctual that he never loses where the puck is, whether he can see it or not. It drives me nuts he's so freaking talented that way.

"Well," we stand, "let's kick ass."

"That's what we're here for."

We make our way off the ice so the puck drop can take place. I glance into the stands and see Callie sitting with a girl beside her. It must be a girlfriend.

It pleases me to have her watch me play until I remember she's here to check out Peety, not me. He needs my help, and I intend to help him in any way I can. I have his back, even if he never knows about this. And if that means kissing up to Callie, I'm up for the task.

12

CALLIE

Electricity fills the air as the crowd chants, "Maulers," repeatedly as we wait for our team to exit the tunnel— strobe blue, white, and purple lights dart about the room.

A beach ball comes our way, and Sarah and I hit it at the same time before we turn to each other and laugh. This reminds me of college football games.

"So, hubby home with the little rug rats?"

"For sure, can't afford a sitter for three kids. Are you kidding me? I don't make what babysitters do per hour!"

"Gee, yeah, I suppose you're right with wages going up everywhere."

"Yep, and thanks for the tickets. This is awesome!"

"I have to say, this is nice sitting so close to the center line."

"He likes you. It's more than just business with him," Sarah adds.

"No, can't be. He's not gonna look at me when he's used to getting models and celebrities. I can't compete with their looks or money."

"Not every guy wants that. Some are low-key and want a salt-of-the-earth type of girl when it comes to settling down. We don't always marry the type we date." She slurps the foam off her beer and gives me a knowing look.

She has a point. I thought my first marriage was perfect and would last forever. We had similar interests and goals. Little did I know his interests included other women, and everything came crashing down.

When I was married, I wanted kids, and I still do. My biological clock is ticking, and the desire for them has my hormones in overdrive. Alexandre is cute and would produce adorable kids.

I like to be in control of my own destiny, and that's another reason it's easier for me not to get involved with someone new and untamed. I find their world to be beyond my comprehension.

However, the long nights are becoming longer. I've had to replace my electric vibrator, and I'm not one who wants to spend my life alone. I don't find sanctuary in being physically alone. I've realized I'm too defensive to attract the right guys because I refuse to allow myself to be in a position to be hurt again.

"Ha." I almost choke on my beer. "In other words, I dated nice guys and married an asshole."

Sarah covers her mouth to avoid spitting her beer into the guy's head sitting in front of her as she struggles to contain her laugh and keep her beer inside her mouth.

"You have a way with words."

The puck drops, and our team fans out, blocking offensive players who want to score. They have all the energy of a cyclone hitting guys off the puck, and then there are the guys falling over sticks because the Sharks did a can opener on a player who was on a breakaway. The two-minute penalty doesn't seem to fit the crime, but many more dirty deeds are up their sleeves.

Our team's momentum is impressive. I take it as a sign we'll do well tonight. Better if we win, we have six more games to go.

Alexandre skates up the boards, short strides at first until he gains speed, switching to longer ones before making a shot-on goal.

I hear the telltale clink when the hard puck makes contact with the crossbar, and the crowd groans with disappointment. The puck bounces behind the goalie and is scooped up by a Shark player, who passes it up the channel, where we intercept it.

We get another shot on goal. My blood pressure is officially off the chart because I'm holding my breath as I sit on the edge of my seat. I'm so swept up in the game and excited about how well we're playing I forget to drink my beer has grown warm waiting for me.

"I hope we score first. If we do, there's a higher statistical probability that we'll win."

"Callie, relax. It's a game, enjoy."

"You know me."

"You need to forget about work and get into the game, feel it, enjoy it. Stop running the numbers."

She's right, and there's no reason to keep working. The staff keeps track of all the stats on the guys. I keep forgetting about Peety because I'm too busy checking Alexandre's moves. As if by some divine intervention, he sends the puck to the top shelf while the goalie is down and scores!

The crowd erupts, and we're both on our feet, screaming with the rest of the fans. I holler, "Way to go Alex!" even though it's futile. There is no way he can hear me down there with all the noise.

He swings by the bench and taps the gloves of his teammates as he cruises by. Their smiles are evident by the number of missing teeth we can see when the Jumbotron camera moves in for a close-up.

Rock music plays, sirens go off, and the announcer calls the player and the score. The fans settle down and sit to wait for the next epic moment.

The new rookie from Wisconsin on the Sharks team, who can skate like a rocket, runs the puck into our zone. With the Sharks changing out a player, the timing is perfect to give him someone to pass to. They both rush in, passing it back and forth and before our players get there, the puck goes under the goalie's crotch.

Damn.

The score comes across the speakers, and the Boston fans go nuts.

1-1.

Shit.

"So, is there anything you left out about your lunch with Alexandre yesterday? What do you know of his hockey school?" Sarah asks while there's a lull in the game.

"Hmm, only what he told me. Probably wanted to make an impression and shake his bad boy image." I shrug.

"I can see that, but still, it counts for something. Kids need to have something constructive to do at any age, especially in their teen years. I worry about keeping my boys busy. As for Susie, she's creative and doesn't like to sweat. I'm happy at age seven, she still thinks boys are gross."

I scoffed, " Wait until she has her first break-up. She may be living with you forever," I tease.

"Hi guys, mind if I join you?"

I look up to find a tall blonde holding a boxed dinner and a beer. "I'm Emily, by the way, Wyatt's fiancé. Alexandre wanted me to stop by."

"Sure, that would be great," Sarah beats me again as the welcoming committee of one.

I smile and flip her seat open so she can sit beside me.

I wondered why there was an empty seat in a sold-out game.

"The guys look good. You must be Callie." She smiles at me as she opens the foil around her burger and sips her beer.

"Yes, I am." The confused look on my face must be prompting her to embellish.

"My fiancé and Alexandre are friends, so I got the jump on the newbie."

"Newbie?" I'm not a newbie at anything. What is she talking about?

"Well, Alexandre didn't want to you to come tonight without meeting some of the WAGS."

"Oh." I get it, the wives and girlfriends. Emily is the older woman I heard about shortly after Wyatt arrived on the team earlier this year.

"Alexandre wanted me to introduce myself. I'm sure you're big girls who can take care of yourselves, but there are some I should warn you about." Raising her eyebrows.

"This is my best friend, Sarah." I smile, appreciating her candor.

"Hi, Sarah, forgive me for not shaking hands." She takes a bite of the burger she has clinched between her hands. Like a game of Jenga, the burger might fall apart at any minute as the tomato and lettuce dangle precariously out of the bun.

"There's something about a burger here," I surmise.

"Mm," Emily murmurs.

Sarah nudges my ribs with a fast elbow jab. I wince and move away.

"What?" I bark quietly at her.

"Told you. You're not really here to watch Peety. Alexandre has a crush on you."

"He'd probably do that for anyone," I whisper.

Between bites of her burger, Emily says, "Y'know, Alexandre is funny. He's never asked me to meet any of his flings here."

Another jab in my ribs, and I use my elbow to nudge Sarah's away, trying to be inconspicuous.

"Is that a fact?" Sarah chirps, encouraging Emily to say more.

"Yep, I mean, I've met some, and they all had an uppity air about them. I can tell you two aren't like that." She flashes me a quick smile before taking another bite of her burger.

"I'm sure he doesn't mean anything special by it. We barely know each other," I drone on.

"Um, yeah, he mentioned that." Her whimsical air stirs my curiosity.

I hope Sarah doesn't jab my ribs again. Her elbows are as sharp as the blade of a skate.

It seems Alexandre is quite the onion as I peel back the layers of his rough exterior. Underneath all that, there's much more that I never gave him credit for.

I look for him on the ice and find him slamming some dude into the boards.

It seems the Tin Man might have a heart after all.

But then again, I'm not Dorothy. And I have a Lucy, not a Toto.

However, Alexandre resembles a lion, one of many in his pack who exudes self-confidence and strength. I'm on the fence about him. His bad reputation and these new pieces to the puzzle don't match up, and it's confusing the hell out of me.

I jump and yell when I see Alexandre on a quick breakaway, but he misses the net. The game's win hangs in the balance as skaters move up and down the ice, and both goalies are blocking every shot.

Looks can be deceiving. I hope to God I'm wrong about Alexandre being a bad boy because I can't wait to see him after the game.

13

ALEXANDRE

Our fans are noisy, and I strain to hear my teammate shout a cue to me, directing me as to where he wants me. I love the rowdy and feisty bunch of fans in the stands, but tonight it hinders our ability to communicate.

I'm getting all the ice time a player wants and more. But the pressure from the other team is hitting us, and my leg muscles' fatigue makes it more difficult to skate as fast as I would in a regular season game.

I welcome the shift change and exit the ice. Our opponents deliver the message that they are as tough as us, which means this will be a physical game. We can't let our foot off the gas if we want to stay alive for game two.

The checking into the boards and poke checks are essential to get possession of the puck. It's a higher level of hockey, and I never understood how much of a difference it is until today.

It's the toughest competition I've ever experienced, and the greatest prize awaits if we are successful in our mission to win at every level. The elimination rounds will take weeks as we play our contemporaries in our division.

Cup winners talk about the hard work at the award ceremonies, but until today, I had no idea what being here would be like, and it's surreal. We take hits, and we deliver our share. Some guys fall hard and are helped off the ice after the whistle is blown. It could be me; it could be any one of us.

The game resumes, and the players on the bench tap their sticks as the injured player leaves the ice to get medical attention: another day, another hit, another attempt at the net.

"Let's go, come on, guys," Peety shouts across the ice, waving a gloved hand for us to pick it up.

The song *High Hopes* is played during a brief lull due to a penalty call and one of our players is sent to the box. I wouldn't consider that hooking, but that's how the dice roll.

We have to overcome bad calls by the refs and a weird puck bounce that might give our opponent a lead. It happens all the time, which is why I hate overtime. I'd rather win the game straight up and as quickly as possible. If I didn't, I don't belong here.

We're on a penalty kill and I wait until our player's two minutes are up before I can get back on the ice. Peety's on the second line and comes to the bench sitting in the order in which he'll return to the game. He gives me a friendly nudge as he passes.

"Hang in there. We can do this."

My gloves are off and a tablet lands in my hands to review our last play. I share it with Sean, AKA Sniper. I hit the play arrow and we watched the formation we just ran and saw how their defense covers us like a shiver of sharks, seriously, they are not called schools. Our opponents have a block method set up around their goalie that is hard to penetrate.

I know the girls are behind me, and as much as I'd love to see Callie, I push her out of my mind. The crush I have on her distracts me. I can't turn around, nor do I want to. This game means life, life to fight another day. First games are all about feeling the other team out but can be particularly sweet if it's a win for us.

For some, it would be the high signaled by a bell going off on a slot machine and all that change coming out. Jackpot! I wouldn't know what that's like because I don't gamble. I don't like taking chances. Callie and I have that in common.

Our penalty kill is over, and it's my turn as three of us head out on the ice at the same time. Our timing is bad, and the Sharks have the puck in our zone before I can get my legs going. I arrive at the net after they get a shot off. It bounces. I dive toward the rolling puck and knock it with my blade as hard as I can. The puck sails into their zone.

Whew! Safe for now.

I quickly get to my feet and take off after it, knowing that a 2-1 score isn't good enough with our opponents who tend to be chippy. A fight breaks out behind their net as the buzzer goes off, effectively ending the first period.

All I can think about is that little shit of a player, Anderson, on the Sharks, who continues to knock me around every chance he gets. He's a huge fucking Swede, and he's about to get his face smashed.

I leave my stick with the equipment manager and shove my gloves in the slots for them to dry out for the next few minutes. We pile into the locker room filled with mixed emotions, happy we have a goal, but knowing it's not good enough. We need to give more, be more and do more.

Our helmets come off, and our hair is wet with sweat, it resembles a child's first attempt at decoupage in school when they try to cover a balloon with glue and paper. Our hair sticks to our faces and necks. Most of the guys grew beards for good luck.

We sit on the bench and hydrate, drinking from one of the numerous bottles around us. We don't worry about spitting; we spit all the time on the ice. We're often covered in blood and have been exposed to every bodily fluid, our own or someone else's, throughout our careers.

Coach enters our 'den' and gives us a pep talk. After he leaves,

Peety stands and starts singing *We're Not Gonna Take It* from the song by Twisted Sister. It breaks the tension in the air because he can't sing a lick and is dancing around using his water bottle as a microphone.

I'm frustrated, but Peety's a character and not afraid to make a fool of himself for a good laugh. He's not afraid to lay it all out there in an attempt to motivate us, and I respect that.

The room's temperature cools us down and teammates move around with encouragement for each other on solid plays. I glance up at the clock—time to head out.

The game is moving in slow motion as we wear each other out, running up and down the boards.

I take to the ice, and this time we're not so lucky as the Shark's leading scorer lobs one into the net. A weird bounce off a player's skate and a tip by his teammate's stick lifts the puck over Luc's thick leg pads.

Tied 2-2.

I tap Luc on the back to reassure him we don't blame him. The fact is goalies are our most revered players. He handles it well, as he always does, but I'm here for him just the same. It means more coming from me right now because I'm not known as Mr. Congeniality on the team.

The score stays at 2-2 until the third period when Wyatt takes a shot at the net, it bounces weirdly, leaving the goalie off to one side of the net and the other side is wide open. Peety is there and easily slaps the puck in, giving us a 3-2 win over the Sharks as the buzzer sounds.

He screams, "Yes!" and he goes down on one knee as he glides over the ice. I'm the second person to reach him, and after that, the entire line engulfs him with our bulky arms as we laugh and congratulate him on the 'W'. The sheer joy of winning is combined with relief because we pulled it off knowing all along that we were the underdogs.

The entire team comes off the bench to high-five and tap our goalie before we leave the ice. The fans are still cheering, and I take a minute to enjoy it, knowing we can be knocked out in four more games.

Peety is the most unlikely hero, but he's the man who saved the day, and we're all smiles as we head to the locker room to celebrate with the rest of our teammates.

Beers are popping and the guys make jokes as loud laughter erupts here and there and the music is drowned out by our excited chatter.

"Way to go, Playoff Pete!" I comment, hugging him again.

The locker room picks up on my new name for him and chants 'Playoff Pete, Playoff Pete' as we peel off our sweat-soaked clothes, rub sore elbows, and tally up the bruises on our torsos. I'm happy Playoff Pete rose to the occasion tonight, of all nights. He doesn't even know that he scored big off the ice as well.

Music is blaring as we shower, down more beers, and pat each other on the back. I have other things on my mind now that the game is over.

I'm one of the first to leave the locker room, in the hope that Emily kept the girls around to celebrate with us at the brew house. We notoriously shut the place down after huge wins like this. Tonight will be no different.

Well, different, in that, we'll make sure we're not hungover for game two and different, in that, I can't wait to see Callie again.

14

CALLIE

Sarah, Emily, and I jump up and down, yelling. I yelled at every attempt we had at scoring in the last period. I've lost my voice. Emily invited us to hang with her so we could see the guys briefly before they left to celebrate.

"I have to go home, but you two go; after all, your guys are on the team," Sarah announces.

"I wouldn't say that," I reply.

"I would." She smiles, hugs me, and heads out.

"Guess it's just us." I look to Emily.

"I have a pass to get through, so let's go down to the main level."

I follow her as we work through swarms of happy people yelling as they leave the arena.

"Oh, here we are." She finds the corridor where security stands in blue suits and security badges.

She flashes a badge from her purse, and we are allowed through. I didn't need a map to find the guys because we could hear them once we came upon another corridor.

Emily pulls her phone out of a designer purse large enough for her phone and minor essentials. She pulls off glam without makeup, her hair is gorgeous, and her messy bun is adorable.

I wish I could look so cool. I'm in skinny jeans, still white sneakers, as I bought them a few weeks ago for summer, and the Maulers jersey with the goalie's name on the back.

Emily is wearing a cute half-sweater, and her jeans have rhinestones. I have no idea where she got them, but I'm sure they would set me back a paycheck.

Wyatt comes out without his jersey, and I recognize him with his dark hair and eyes, but the beard throws me for a loop.

"Hey, babe." He kisses Emily on her perfect lips and lingers longer than just a 'hello' before he glances at me. "Hi, you must be Callie." He shakes my hand.

I give him a questioning look.

"I play with Alexandre, don't sweat it. Besides, I know he wanted Emily to keep you company."

"True," Emily volunteers.

"Oh, well, yeah." I wonder what kind of network they have, as they are more efficient than a beehive which is astonishing.

I assumed men are not efficient and social engagement outside their favorite pub would be non-existent. I guessed wrong.

Alexandre shows up, and his face is scruffy. He must be growing a beard for good luck, even though the others have a few months start on him.

"Hi, what a game," Emily says.

They intend to make me comfortable, but I'm not in their league, and meeting more players is, well . . . incredible.

"Look, you want to celebrate, so have fun. We'll talk later," I say.

"You sure?"

"Of course."

Wyatt gives Emily another kiss, and I notice the rock on her ring finger and remember they got engaged this spring.

"See ya' later." Wyatt returns to the guys.

Emily and I head out of the arena together.

"That was cool."

"Yeah, I love seeing Wyatt after a game. They are sweaty and smelly, but it's part of the gig, y'know?"

"Hum, I'm new to this. I've never even skated."

"Oh, well, that's fine."

We continue through the parking lot, and I'm looking for my Jeep as Emily asks to exchange phone numbers so we can hang out sometime.

"Sure." I type her name in my phone, and she does the same, but I don't expect to hear from her. She's sweet, and if we met up by chance, maybe we'd be friends, but Alexandre and I aren't together, yet no one is grasping this huge detail. They assume I'm one of them.

Emily hugs me and walks off to her car in another direction.

Alexandre will say I told you so as soon as he can. I have no doubts on this as I drive home. I take Lucy out and get ready for bed with my two-piece pajama set in pink made of cotton. I open my bedroom window so I can feel the cool evening breeze. The humidity is low tonight, and the moving air is a benefit of living in a rural area.

The incredible night ends with me alone in bed, and I know the wives and girlfriends are doing the same thing. The guys will be out all night, I gather. I assume from comments I heard, as I've never been a part of the in-crowd before.

The women will be taken care of at another juncture on the journey to the Cup. Of that, I am certain.

I toss and turn, not able to fall asleep, wishing I was out with the guys to celebrate their hard-earned victory.

But I have to work in the morning, and the guys don't.

Sarah is jazzed when I walk into the office.

"That was amazing. My husband was a bit peeved that I went to the game and not him."

"Tough cookies." I don't give in to the martyr role he likes to use to make her feel guilty about enjoying a night out with me.

"Tell me about it." She rolls her eyes.

I'm wondering if her home life is all that due to her recent comments and roving comments about her boss. Is she shopping for an upgrade?

"I couldn't sleep last night."

"Did you go out?"

"No, only the guys, you know, the," and I make air quotes, "team."

"Gotcha, so the division of team VS the WAGS."

"Yup. Wives and girlfriends are the backbone of men's lives, and their celebrations are different. For all I know, the wives did something, but Emily went home."

"Emily is sweet, and from what I hear, she fundraises for us. She's not like the stereotyped snobbish women in that group."

"Hum, really?"

"Yeah, I bet that's why Alexandre had her meet up with us. You'd be running for the hills if you ran into some of those other women first."

"Wow, I never thought about that, but you're right." A few choice social media posts come to mind. I do not know their hidden agendas, but I hope I'm not sucked into the drama.

On a positive note, I'm feeling better.

"What's in your box?"

"Mitch's jacket."

"Hum, growing up, I see," she muses as she glances down at her agenda for the day.

"I'll send it out from here. It's time to move on and all that. I can't believe it's taken me this long to make it final."

"Tell me about it, but you're here now, and there's going to be a happy ending for you, you'll see."

"Are you happy?"

"Sure," she says, but from the way she's not looking at me, I have my doubts.

Her phone rings, so I go to my office just as my cell phone goes off.

"Good morning, how are 'ya?"

"Fine. I'm surprised you're up this early."

"Hell, I haven't been to bed yet. I'm just getting in."

I'm surprised to be on his mind after a night of debauchery. "Well, sleep well."

"How are you doing?"

"Loved the game. Thanks for the seats. Emily is a sweetheart, and I'm sending the ex his leather jacket right now."

"Progress, that's great." His voice becomes invigorated, then fades like tired air.

"Yep. New day, new me."

"Alright, I'll let you get to it, and yeah, I have to say, Playoff Pete saved the day. It's not all about the numbers."

"It was one game; this is a marathon, and I have to look at next year."

"Yeah, yeah, we'll see. Later."

"Bye."

His plug wasn't beating me over the head, and I knew I'd hear it eventually.

Sure, I love my numbers, and he doesn't know I can tell there is more than just the CORSI formula. However, hockey is slowly trending into a combination of old and new ways.

But it's fun to give him shit over it.

15

ALEXANDRE

I didn't get as hammered as the other guys because I wanted to make a good impression on Callie. Plus, I don't want to nurse a hangover when I wake up. We've all built up a tolerance to alcohol over the years. As happy as we are with the win, the fact that Callie was there to see me play made the night special.

Knowing this is our first round and we're at home makes this win all that more important because we're not the best team on the road. Some teams play better on away games or during the third period when they consistently come from behind and win, but we're still in that undecided area, where it can go either way.

The home-ice advantage is huge for us because we have an arena filled with screaming fans, and it gives us energy. We love our fans.

After a robust night out with the guys eating bar food, drinking beer and liquor, I fall into my pillow. I arrive home exhausted. I need sleep. I call Callie early in the morning to tell her good night because she's on my mind in my minute of glory, and I can't wait to see her again.

Later I will hydrate and eat protein and carbs to feed the muscles, especially my legs and arms. I run the risk that my muscles will tighten up in a game if I don't keep moving them. Even now, they still have that weird jittery feeling from the fatigue, and my body is sore from being checked into the boards and more than a few as our opponents tried to ride me off the puck.

Last night the mission of the Sharks was to target our best-scoring players. They were gunning for me all night, evidenced by the pain in my side and bruises on my back.

And rightfully so, we'd do the same, but not to inflict an injury bad enough to sideline a player. It got out of control quickly when the Sharks got frustrated, and a few fights broke out. I let the other guys take care of it because the team can't afford to have me in the penalty box. Sometimes I'll get involved, but I tried to behave last night.

I ignored the rude comments and remained focused on the task at hand to get to the puck. It was an uphill battle all night, and it's not likely to get any easier in the next game.

Exhausted, I have no trouble sleeping. When I wake, I'm as hungry as a bear coming out of hibernation. I burned tons of calories last night and am still in a caloric deficit.

I bust out my air-fryer to grill some chicken and fresh veggies to tide me over until dinner. I texted Callie, and she texted back. Weird that we haven't even shared a kiss, but I can picture her here with me.

I sigh. Eating alone is the downside to living alone.

Living the single life may appear to be all fun and games, but it's not all it's cracked up to be unless you have a lone-wolf personality. People may say that's me, but deep in my heart, I know I'm not that guy.

I text Callie again and ask her to join me for dinner after she's off work. I would call her, but I don't want to interrupt her at work.

My phone dings, and in my eagerness to read her answer, I lunge to grab it, nearly knocking the air fryer into the sink.

Sure, gotta celebrate the win.

Yes, we do.

Can I pick up after work?

Sure. What time?

7 p.m.

She sends her address, and it's not far away. Camden Hills and Camden Bay are nice areas and well-known. This area is small, so anyone who has lived here for over a year knows the local neighborhoods. We don't have a huge downtown or sprawling burbs like the metropolitan areas further up the coastline.

With no tall buildings around it, our capital building in Augusta can be seen for miles. Anyone can put their arm out their car window while driving past and touch it. The capital of Maine is that small, no joke.

So I have a date.

I flip my chicken onto a plate and retrieve the cooked veggies from the bottom of the air fryer. I could use a huge fatty steak to help absorb the alcohol I consumed last night. There is no harm in eating more calories, so dinner at a great steak house is a good idea. All I need to do is make a reservation.

I want to know more about Callie, and for the first time, I use social media to investigate her. I enjoy the fact I don't have to leave the comfort of my kitchen to do so. I'm not proud of my actions, but my inner voices don't stop me from snooping online.

Some accounts are private, but in the pictures I find are of her dog or friends. The dog and Callie are cute, but a light in her eyes is missing. It's a darkness that I have noticed growing into a light of hope, maybe even a hint of genuine happiness with her moving on from her ex-husband. I'd like to see the glassy shine in my eye that I get when I think about playing hockey.

I wonder if her job brings her joy as much as mine does. She appears to like the outdoors. I do, too. I mean, we're both in Maine.

I can't imagine why she's single unless she still has her defenses up when it comes to men because she's afraid of getting hurt again.

Maybe it's the comfort of being on the sidelines. I wonder which one it is or if it's a bit of both.

Maybe it's easier for her to hide. Just like I skirt the media, she avoids men. Finishing my food, I use my phone to book a restaurant with great reviews. Can't go wrong with surf and turf and a nice bottle of wine. Mission accomplished, I decided to jump in the pool for an afternoon swim to loosen up.

I wear my silver Audemars Piguet with a blue face to get dressed for dinner. I have plenty of nice watches, but this is my favorite. Watches remind me of my grandfather and how he came to all my practices and games as I was growing up.

In fact, I still have the watch he wore, a Timex with a leather band. Before he passed, he gave me my first watch, and now I'm an avid collector. Yes, I have expensive taste, but it's an indulgence I can afford.

~

AFTER A SHORT DRIVE, I approach Callie's two-story Cape Cod-style house. It sits on what looks to be a half-acre with a nicely manicured lawn in the front and woods in the back. It's an old house built when ladies needed to escape the heat indoors and sat outside on porches sipping tea or lemonade. The house blends nicely with the surrounding area, just like it did one-hundred years ago.

Maine has an abundance of these older homes, but due to the poor economy, most of them are not up to health and safety codes, yet people still live in them.

These are not the types of homes you will see in my gated community, but they have character. Her place is so historical, like the old-fashioned horse and buggy days, that my car is a spaceship in comparison.

Callie opens the screen door as I walk over the cracked sidewalk. Before I can reach her, a large yellow lab runs over to me.

Cock blocked by a dog, that's a first, I muse as I glance down at Callie's best friend, who is sniffing my pant legs and shoes.

I lean over to greet her dog; it's clear that Callie's personal life is filled with love from the purebred as I rub her back, and she nuzzles up to me.

"That's Lucy." Her sweet voice greets me as the screen doors swing shut behind her, reminding me of my grandparent's house in Quebec.

"Hi, Lucy." I continue petting her as we climb the porch steps together. Callie is leaning on the railing and looks radiant.

She no longer has the helpless I'm-sulking-over-losing-Mitch look anymore. This isn't the same woman I met earlier this week. Today, she's confident, shoulders back, her hair in an updo, and she's wearing a knee-length blue and white paisley dress that blows gently on the evening breeze.

It's sleeveless, and the neckline shows off her cleavage perfectly. The dress is casual but not on her. No, anything on her is noticeable because she's wearing it.

"Want to come in?"

"You look gorgeous."

"I don't think so, but thanks for saying that." Her modesty overtakes any compliment again as she opens the door.

"Don't sell yourself short. I think you have a hard time taking a compliment."

"Maybe," she says, letting Lucy inside.

"We have some time before the reservation," I nervously add.

Why did I do that? I'm not a schoolboy. She makes me a bit nervous. She's above swooning at my feet just because I'm a jock.

We're close enough that a kiss wouldn't be amiss if we knew each other longer. I'm tempted to drop a seductive one on her bubble gum-colored lips because that is what I want, but in my gut, I'm afraid I'll scare her off like a baby rabbit who will scamper into the underbrush at the first sign of danger.

It will be better received later, so I stop myself.

I want her to want me. I want to see her breathless, waiting for my lips to meet hers in a first kiss. A kiss we'll remember when our hair is gray and we're watching the grandkids climb the apple trees in her front yard.

And at this moment, standing in her house, I realize she's the reason I've never fallen in love before. The others weren't right.

Sure, I never said a girl's name before, but does that give my heart immunity? Was I kidding myself?

Now I understand what the women who fell in love with me must have experienced in their unrequited love. And I won't be happy until Callie wants me like I want her.

My heart flutters. Weird, I didn't know guys could have the same symptoms of lust, a crush, or the inklings of love . . . is it possible that I am experiencing palpitations in my chest? Anxiety?

She turns to stroll through the house, leaving a peach scent in her wake, and I follow her like a bloodhound.

"This isn't much, but I've been restoring the house, finishing up where the prior owners left off a few years ago," she explains.

The first thing I notice is the original hardwood floors that are shiny, and my shoes make a clicking sound as I walk. It's a beautiful floor made from Maple trees and a wax seal that shines as it winds up the ornate staircase with a matching wooden banister. The ceiling has been dropped to that of a typical house, and two wood-burning fireplaces grace the living quarters, and they quite possibly run up to the rooms above.

"This is incredible," I keep repeating as she shows me around the house. With its recessed lighting and granite countertops, the modern kitchen looks much different from 100 years ago. But she's pulled it off as old-world charm meets new-world function.

I look out the window over the sink, see another long porch off the back, and feel a sense of déjà vu. I've never had that happen with a girl before.

"This is a stunning place."

"Thanks."

I realize now that it's easier for her to take a compliment on her work or her house than her beauty, which adds to her charm.

"Can I get you a drink?"

"Oh, no, thanks. Really. I hope you are in the mood for an incredible steak dinner. I have a great place reserved."

"I think you are spoiling me, and it might raise some eyebrows if Peety is traded."

"There's no policy against us dating."

"No, but I wouldn't want anyone to think he received preferential or unfair treatment because we're seeing each other."

"I take it 'we're seeing each other' means we're more than friends," I take the plunge to find out more, and it's not out of arrogance that I'm so curious.

"Maybe." She can't stop a demure grin that reaches her eyes.

It's a sign that I'm making points. This is good.

I wait while she pets Lucy goodbye.

"Alright then. Let's enjoy the night and our win. Eh?"

"Sure."

I can tell she's comfortable with me now as she takes my hand so I can escort her down the porch steps in her high heels. I want to scoop her up and carry her to bed, but I'll save that impulse for later.

16

CALLIE

His long strides reach the porch before I have time to prepare for him standing next to me. There's plenty of room, but he makes no attempt to give me space. His magnetic presence sucks me to the point I'm breathless.

I try not to notice the sparks of chemistry between us, and judging by the looks of it, he's experiencing the same issue. He's shoved his hands in his trouser pockets as if it's the only way to keep them from touching me.

Maybe he is interested in me. Lunch was just that, but going out for an expensive dinner is another animal altogether.

He's wearing a long-sleeved shirt rolled up to his elbows, showing off his muscular forearms, and a beautiful watch that looks expensive.

His cologne reminds me of something from my past, but I can't put my finger on it. Is it real or imagined? I can't tell. He reminds me of a part of my life that I wasn't living to the fullest. Now, I find myself wanting more.

Damn him for turning my world upside down. Between the sexy accent he pours on when he wants to and his hard body, it's difficult to resist him. I hate fishing, but if he touched me right now, I'd be lost, hook, line, and sinker.

I hesitate, anticipating his lips touching mine with just a dip of his head. However, when he doesn't move, I sigh in disappointment.

To smooth over the awkwardness, I invite him to come inside. He hesitates a second; then he turns to follow me. I show him around my home, nervous that I might have given away the fact that he drives me crazy. Did he catch the uptick in my breathing?

Did I scare him off by telling him too much about myself?

I know I did.

Damnit.

I never know when to stop talking, especially when the person I'm with is quiet. But Alexandre, he listens to me. He internalizes everything I've shared with him about my divorce. That alone terrifies me. I love the way he listens intensely when I speak.

I'm in over my head with this professional hockey player/playboy. I should run now or tell him some deep secret about myself that will make him bolt.

But I come up empty.

Having already played that card, I have nothing left.

When I watch him staring out in my kitchen window, the only thought on my mind is that he has heartache written all over him.

He's never had a relationship that lasted more than a year. For a man his age, that's not a good sign. But I haven't had a date in over a year, and that's a red flag, too.

He compliments me on the house, and I'm glad he likes it. I wish I could feel the same way when he says sweet things about me. Instead, I feel anxious and overwhelmed and don't know what to say. It's a good thing there's a dog around to focus on during these awkward segways.

We both pat Lucy's head before we leave the house.

As we drive, the sky is clear, and the sun is showing off its impressive colors of yellow and pink. It's the perfect sunset.

"You sure live in the country. What brought you back to Maine?"

"So you've been doing your homework, huh?" I can't let that pass without giving him shit over it.

"Um, yeah, well, I have to know my opposition."

"I'm opposition?" I question the word he uses to avoid calling this a date.

"Right. Well, I just wanted to know more about you," he explains, "you are beautiful, you know."

I'm looking at him when he turns to me, and I'm sure he understands that any woman would be defenseless against his charm. And his body, well, that's a given.

The result is that I'm horny and wondering what it would be like if he just reached over and . . .

"I hope you like steak." He breaks the intense moment I'm struggling over. Our hearts touched for a second, but like a shooting star, it flared up like a shooting flame and burned out just as quickly.

What didn't go away was the tingling of warmth between my legs that I hadn't experienced in a long time. Too long. I want him to touch me and imagine his hands running down my sides, my hips, and my thighs and chastise myself for even thinking he could be interested in me, the woman who has her head stuck in spreadsheets and computer programs.

However, I can't get him off my mind at work. And overnight, he's become my latest addiction, a part of my day I look forward to as much as I do my break time with Sarah and my cup of coffee from Luke's.

I sneak a peek at his lap when his eyes are on the road. I'm satisfied he's also feeling our attraction when I take in the bulge in his trousers.

I try to keep the talk in neutral territory because if he makes a move, I'd so do him in this sports car. I shudder at how hot that would be. There's more room in a phone booth, but he's so doable. Sarah said it first, and even though she's been acting off lately, she has good taste in men and what they desire.

I smile and stare at his profile, the way his chin juts out and his composure is perfectly . . . Alexandre. It dawns on me that I'm in the same pond with a man named Alexandre Holloway, and I'm no longer on the sidelines.

After forty minutes, we arrive at the coast and stop at a swanky restaurant. I quickly Google the place's name and see it's a five-star restaurant. What have I got myself into? This is a luxury I've only had on my honeymoon.

I look around and surmise that I'm underdressed when the hostess looks prettier than me with her makeup perfect and long lashes on her eyelids. If she's judging my choice of attire, she doesn't let it show as she leads us to the rooftop, where we're greeted with a majestic view of the Atlantic Ocean. It's turning darker as the sunlight fades, and soon, the impending darkness will comfort us with the salty air and the comfort of a handmade quilt on a cold winter night.

"Perfect timing," the hostess says as she seats us. A cool salty ocean breeze engulfs us as the sun dips lower.

"Great, it's been a long time since I've been here," Alexandre answers as he pulls out my chair. The hostess leaves us with menus and moves on to greet other guests.

"How come?"

"Busy, and my ex is from Canada, so we were there more during summer than here. I guess it was here and there, but rarely were we in the same place long enough to have any semblance of what a real relationship would be like together."

"Oh, yeah, how is Canada? I've never been."

"Small town, rural." He raises one eyebrow as if I should know this.

"No idea. I'm not an expert on Canada."

"Right, well, I have a sister in Quebec who visits from time to time. It's pretty far north, and we speak our dialect of French."

This helps to explain his arrogance. I read somewhere that the French prefer English-speaking foreigners to speak English rather than butcher their French.

"Does your sister have a name?"

"Oh, yeah, Rachel. She's sweet. We're like two peas in a pod, only she hasn't found her calling yet."

"Blogger?"

"How did you know?"

"Seems to fit somehow." I smile demurely.

"You do surprise me; I'd never guess that in a million years."

"She's younger than you, right?"

"Yes, why?"

"It's the age. I picture her as a sweet girl with the newest phone glued to her hand."

"Pretty much." His smile turns me inside out.

The server introduced herself and suggested the best wine for our steak dinner. We decide on a red blend, and Alexandre doesn't even ask how much it is. I guess the price is inconsequential when you want the best and can well afford it.

We toast to the team's win as the horizon displays the colors of the perfect sunset. It occurred to me that I could get used to this.

17

———

ALEXANDRE

Callie sips her wine, and a cool breeze glides over us as we walk to the rooftop's side for a better view of the setting sun. Instinctively, I put my arm around her bare shoulders to protect her, and my body comes alive when I come in contact with her soft skin and toned arms.

She leans her head against my chest as if we've known each other for years, and her peach shampoo mixes with the salty air. It reminds me of a liqueur in a drink my mother loves called Sex on the Beach. Ironically, it's something I wouldn't mind doing right now.

The more I get to know her, the more I realize how similar we are. The fact that she's a local is new to me and oddly comforting. She's the first woman I've been with since high school who doesn't crave the spotlight.

We stand watching the waves bang into the rocks below us. Chinese lanterns light up as they are strung over our heads, and it creates a pleasant ambiance.

Behind us is an outdoor seating area of wicker chairs and couches with red cushions for guests to mingle with cocktails.

We finish the last sips of our wine, and I take her empty glass from her as we return to our table, where another server promptly refills them, and another brings us an appetizer of portobello mushrooms stuffed with fresh lobster. She's enjoying the culinary excursion. Her cheeks glow, not from the soft ambient light, but from pleasure.

My lusty thoughts are interrupted when our main course, chateaubriand, arrives, and we toast to the Mauler's win before diving into the decadent beef and sides large enough to feed me for two days.

I feed her a piece of mashed potatoes, and she gives me a taste of her creamed spinach. It's sensual, inviting, and makes my cock stir under the table. Does she know she's driving me crazy, or is she oblivious to how much I want to take her right here?

A move that would get us both fired, so I hold my cock in the stable like a good man and hope that I don't have to go home alone.

We chuckle over Playoff Pete's new name, and a dessert we didn't even order arrives. A chocolate torte, and yes, I wouldn't say I like chocolate, but I can't say no when Callie's eyes light up. I believe my eyes are shining as brightly upon her as she looks at me to ensure it's okay to sample the decadent dessert.

I'd rather not tell her how I feel about chocolate. I mean, I do eat it on occasion. Who doesn't?

She takes the initiative of picking off a tiny piece of the cake, ensuring it has raspberry sauce, and feeding it to me as our eyes meet. It melts in my mouth, and I lick my lips as my X-rated thoughts turn to what I'd rather be doing with that raspberry sauce.

I take the fork from her hand with French-manicured fingers and feed her a bite.

Our eyes meet again; this time, I lean across the table and claim her lips with mine. The after-set of the sun fills the sky with pink and yellow colors, making it the perfect setting for our first kiss. My cock strains to be released, like a horse at the starting gate, only I want to enjoy the ride and not race to the finish.

I ask for the check, and we leave the restaurant, grabbing some peppermints on the way out. I unwrap mine and place it in her mouth, making sure my fingers touch her warm lips as the hair on the back of my neck stands at attention as if lightning is about to strike.

We arrive at the car, where she unwraps her mint, puts it on her tongue, and kisses me, sliding it into my mouth like a pro. Leaning on the passenger door, my body presses against hers. I'm so turned on I could pull my dick out and take her here and now, pushing her back against the side of my Porsche.

Instead, I run my hand up her thigh, under her lacy panties, and touch her inner lips as our kiss deepens, and her wetness makes it easy for me to slide my fingers inside her, where my cock wants to be. It takes all my fortitude to hear her moan and writhe under my touch and not take her hard and fast in public. She brings out the naughty side in me without any words.

No, I decided our first time has to be special—tender, slow.

I pull my fingers out and lick them, tasting her sweetness.

"We have to go. I'm not doing this here." Sliding my arm behind her to open the car door. "It's bad enough I'm so hard. I don't know how I'm going to get in the car."

She glides her hand over my hard cock, and I suck my breath to keep from exploding.

Fuck, how did this happen? First, I say her name, now she's driving me wild when I thought I was seducing her.

As soon as we're back on the road, she runs her hand across my boner and unfastens her seatbelt. The damn warning bells chime, but that doesn't stop her from unzipping my pants and taking my huge cock in her mouth as she leans over me.

I planned for a hot night but never dreamed it would start on the car ride home. Pleasure surges through my veins like brandy on steroids, and goosebumps ripple down my arms as I grip the steering wheel, clenching my fists around it as I try to focus on the road.

"Ah," I moan.

She's driving me fucking crazy. And I could tell by her demeanor that she knew exactly what she was doing to me.

She runs her tongue up and down my shaft before giving my head extra attention. I hold back coming.

"To be continued," she whispers, putting my hard cock back in the barn and reconnecting her seatbelt.

At the risk of getting a ticket, I drive like the wind back to her place, where we pass fresh-cut grass before we bound up the porch steps, giggling like teenagers as we hold hands.

Once inside, she flips on the lights and lets Lucy out to do her thing. After a few minutes, Lucy returns, and I drop kisses on Callie's smooth neck, running my tongue up to her ear, nibbling on it, and gently blowing into it.

I scoop her up and, with one hand on the banister, carry her up the stairs to the landing, where I put her down, and we race each other to her bedroom.

She helps me with the buttons on my shirt and unzips my pants, tearing off my clothes like wrapping paper on Christmas morning. I unzip her dress, which floats to the floor as I unhook her bra, revealing her voluptuous breasts in the moonlight.

I grab one and play with her button-size nipple, feeling it grow hard with my touch.

She pulls my boxers down and grabs my engorged cock and ass cheeks simultaneously. My gluteus muscles are so hard from years of skating she could bounce a quarter off them.

Her nails dig in, and a groan of pleasure escapes me before I cover her nipple, sucking on it before I grab her other breast, squeezing it and listening to her moan with pleasure.

Tipping her back on the bed, I gaze at her beautiful naked body for a minute. I want to caress, lick, and claim every inch of it as mine.

Her hands caress my sinewy arms, ripped with flexed muscles as I move over her, teasing her with my cock's large head. She tugs my hair, pulls my lips to hers, and demands, "Take me now."

"You sure?" I tease.

She gives me a pretend slap to my cheek, and her lips press harder on mine as I slam my cock inside her, unable to hold myself in check. She's so wet it's like a slip-and-slide ride.

"God damn, you're wet."

"Super excitable personality," she replies.

What the fuck is that?

It doesn't matter, I'm balls deep in her, and we grind on each other until she requests to be on top, where she rides me like the thoroughbred I am, and when this woman comes, she comes hard and fast, crying out in pleasure as wave after wave of orgasms passes through her, constricting her muscles around my cock.

When I'm convinced she's satisfied, I let out a long groan and explode, coming hard from all the prolonged excitement.

Fuck me, a guy can get used to this. How do relationships work? Are we in one? Does she like me, or does she want to have a story to tell her best friend?

18

———

CALLIE

The dinner is exquisite, and the sex is mind-blowing. The animal attraction to him is so overwhelming, and the intense experience makes me wonder if I ever loved Mitch. These feelings are foreign to me. And yet, I can't get enough.

After numerous rounds before dawn, I feel like I'm in college again with the same sexual appetite I've had locked in a box for far too long.

The thrill of being with him, and having his complete attention is worth the risk of a broken heart. The evening was perfect, and he made me feel pretty, successful, and . . . wanted.

I fall asleep, curled up next to him with my head on his muscular chest. It's unclear what the morning will bring. And if it's a one-nighter, I don't want to ruin the perfect evening now.

There was no time to discuss what we wanted from this, his objectives, or even if he likes kids. He likes Lucy; the same Lucy is asleep on the rug next to his side of the bed. Not mine.

Traitor.

Well, at least Alexandre is dog-approved.

What will Sarah say?

I WAKE to a kiss on my lips.

"Morning, Sweetie," he quips.

"Ah." I open my eyes, and my brain runs a spreadsheet on the odds of this being a one-and-done. "Oh, shit, what time is it?" I ask, sitting up and leaning on one elbow to reach for my phone that's not on the nightstand like a normal night.

I forgot to set the alarm on my phone. The phone that's in my purse downstairs.

"You have time to get to work. I'm jazzed from the night. Maybe it was the chocolate?"

"Oh, revs up your energy?"

"Something like that." The crooked grin on his face leads me to believe I'm his new-found flavor.

"Can I get you coffee? I saw the machine downstairs?" His offer is endearing.

"That would be great." I throw back the sheet, hop out of bed, and go to the shower as Alexandre disappears.

After a quick rinse, I dry off just in time for my sexy barista to hand me a piping hot cup of java, wearing nothing more than his boxers.

He's a keeper. No wonder women want him even though I've heard he's sometimes a bit of an ass.

I don't know where this is going. I didn't pepper him with twenty-one questions before falling into a night of pent-up lust.

He kisses my lips, then my shoulder, stirring urges inside me, but I don't have time.

"Ugg, if only it were the weekend." I kiss him quickly, sip my coffee, and grab the nearest dress from my closet because it's fast and easy. I can't make major decisions now.

"It is Friday, though. Do you want the same seat for tonight's game?"

"Awesome, thanks." Turning so he can zip my dress. It's nice not to dislocate a shoulder to zip my dress.

"Maybe Playoff Pete will have another stellar game," he says, leaning against the door jamb to the bathroom and watching me apply makeup.

"Funny how quickly it went from Peety to that."

"Hey, a guy makes a game-winning goal when we need a clutch player to produce, and the most unlikely guy on the team accomplishes it for us."

"Ha, that means you admit we could have a stronger player on the team."

"I think he's safe. He made the game-winning goal." His grin turns me inside out, and I know he's enjoying this debate.

"Don't get your hopes up," I warn.

"No problem. I'm just saying." He returns to the bedroom, tugging on his trousers from last night and picking up his wrinkled shirt that no doubt still wears the scent of his cologne.

"One ticket tonight or two?" he asks, zipping his pants before sliding his belt through them while I sit on the end of the bed to fasten my sandals.

"Two would be great. My co-worker Sarah would enjoy another night out without her three kids."

"Oh," he chuckles, "three? Wow."

"Yeah, tell me about it. They are cute kids, though. She's been kinda off lately. I can't tell what's up with her."

"Something bad?"

"I don't think so. She's like eyeing guys and making comments, and it's not like her. She's a straight arrow. Although she did push me to start dating again."

"Hm, is that what we're doing?" he asks, glancing my way and raising an eyebrow.

My face heats up, and I hope it's not like the Asian Flush I sometimes get when drinking wine that doesn't agree with me.

I put the back of my hand to my cheek as if I could feel how it looks. I'm being silly. I can't use logic or reason with this man so close to me.

"Is this a discussion, or are we labeling it?"

"Either."

His freaking answers aren't helping the situation. What is the winning response? Do I say casual because that's what he probably wants?

What if he doesn't want to date? What if he only does casual? What if this all ends after the playoffs? Or before?

"That's a deflection if I ever heard one." And like that, I'm not in a box anymore.

"Well, we're not kids. I'd say we're a thing." He shrugs, grabbing his wallet from the nightstand and stuffing it in his back pocket.

"Okay." I can play it cool.

"Okay? That's all I get?" he teases, putting on his watch, a brand I've never heard of, but it must be costly as the guys were looking at his watch. The girls at the restaurant were drooling over him, too.

"For now." I'll keep him on his toes and deliver the message that he's still on probation.

"Ouch." But the smirk he's trying to suppress tells me he's enjoying the banter and might be up for the challenge.

"Dating policy at work?" he asks, grabbing his keys from the nightstand before his phone.

"Now that, I'm not sure of. But I don't want to hide our relationship either. I doubt the team would know where I work anyway." I stand, finally buckling my sandal after three attempts because his body distracts me.

"Damn, I'm hungry," he declares as we head downstairs. "It's all that bedroom action."

"No doubt, and also why my thighs and legs are giving me grief today," I add.

He chuckles.

"I take that as a sign I delivered an acceptable performance last night?"

"Now you're fishing for compliments to which you already know the answer."

"Aw, come on. Throw me a bone here."

I let Lucy out and feed her. She knows I'm leaving as soon as I pick up my purse and gives me a pouty face and sad eyes.

"Back soon, girl." I pet her head.

"Bye, girl." Alexandre rubs her back a few seconds before we shut the door behind us.

"I'll look for you in the stands. Tickets will be at will call," he says, opening my car door.

"Thank you."

He leans in for a kiss goodbye, a kiss that makes my fatigued muscles buckle under me, and it takes all my willpower to keep from falling.

"You look radiant."

"Thanks," I say, and for a fleeting moment, I don't want him to leave. I internalize his compliment, and I let it resonate for the first time in my life. He thinks I'm pretty.

Then I slip into old habits and brush it off. I'm nothing compared to his ex-girlfriends.

He slides a hand behind my neck to cup my head and stares into my eyes. "You're beautiful, Callie. You should take the compliment seriously. You are worthy of everything good in life."

"I . . ." I writhe under his bold, dark eyes, taking me in and divert mine.

It's just that I'm a simple girl who never fits in, and this freaking hotter than fuck guy notices me for me. He sees who I am.

"Okay," I softly reply, and when my eyes meet his, I'm overwhelmed by the raw emotion in his.

"Alright." He quickly kisses my lips, and I slide into my car. But when I turn the ignition on, it doesn't start.

"Oh, shit."

"Must be your battery. Do you have a service for that?"

"No." My car has a hundred thousand miles on it, but batteries only last three years.

"Let me give you a ride; give me your keys, and I'll take care of it."

"You don't have to do that."

"I want to, no worries. Let's go."

Alexandre drops me off at the arena and asks when he can pick me up to go home. I mention around five, but I'll text him.

It's not a walk of shame into the office, but Sarah will give me that 'I told you so' look.

I look for her at her desk. She's not there. That's weird. She's always at work before me.

I glance around, but there is no sign of her. After dropping my purse at my desk, I double back and head to the bathroom.

I push the door open and hear someone vomiting in one of the bathroom stalls. I can tell by the heels under the door it's her in there getting sick.

"Sarah, are you alright?"

"Yep." She flushes and opens the door. "Nothing seven more months won't cure."

"Um, baby number four?" I meekly let the obvious words out for her.

"Yeah." Her flat response tells me everything.

"I couldn't figure out what was going on with you. You were checking out guys like you wanted to relive your youth, and it was getting weird."

"Hormones, sorry I worried you." She rinses her mouth in the sink.

"Gee, what's the hubs think?"

"Guilty for not getting the vasectomy I told him to get."

"Oh."

"Yeah. I'm not prepared for another one. I thought we were done. I was looking forward to having a personal life in a few years. I'll be in my fifties by the time this one gets out of high school."

"Hey, I don't have one yet, so if it happens, I'll be in the same boat with you. And you are going to love this kid as much as the others. It might be another girl, and you'll have two of each."

A weak smile crosses her face. "You're a good friend, Callie."

"Of course, I wouldn't have it any other way. You're my sister. BFF isn't cutting it anymore." I hug her.

"Thanks. I don't know what I'd do without you."

"You'd be fine no matter what. Are you feeling better?" I hand her a paper towel.

"Yeah, thanks. I need to get back to work. I'm going to wait before I say anything."

"My lips are sealed."

"So, hot date last night? You look like a woman who has had her brains fucked out."

"OMG, outrageously so." I strain to keep my voice from squealing.

"You like him. He's an arrogant French Canadian, but I think he likes you."

"Time will tell. We're like 'official,'" I add, making air quotes with my fingers. "My car battery died today. He says he's handling it. How does a hockey player change a car battery?"

"Credit card." She giggles as we swing through the double doors and get to work.

"Well, I hope you can go to the game with me tonight!"

Nothing speaks volumes more than a hormonal pregnant woman who has a night out without the entire family.

19

ALEXANDRE

Call me a poser, but I know when I look good. And right now, I look smokin' hot leaning against the side of my Porsche, arms folded, showing off my ripped biceps in a black T-shirt one size too small. Some habits die hard.

"Well, instead of dine and dash, it's a pickup, deliver, and dash," I call out to Callie as she leaves work and approaches me, looking sexy in a cute summer dress.

By the looks of her older car and renovated home, she's not into flashy things like pretty boys and sports cars, but how can she resist me? I'm probably not what she's used to, but I plan to take it slow and get her used to life in the spotlight and under a microscope. I'm not giving up on her and maybe, just maybe, I scored some points last night.

I can still feel the sting of scratch marks on my back, but I wear them proudly, equating them with validation in the bedroom. I work hard on my body, and all the conditioning helps me with stamina and stellar moves between the sheets. I know I'm doing something right when my heart races like a marathon runner.

Callie surprised me last night. I pegged her as reserved, even shy in bed, but her eager participation gave me a preview of a wild side I didn't expect. Maybe she's not all work and no play after all.

I can't believe I agreed for us to be a 'thing.' I'm unsure if it was the euphoria of the night we spent together, the fact that she was growing on me, or if I was telling her what she wanted to hear.

Pulling her into my arms and against my hard abs, I ask, "You set for tonight?"

"Yes, someone got me tickets to a playoff game, and I can't wait," she teases, melting against my hardness like butter on toast. She has no clue what I would give for the opportunity to lay her across the hood and lick her all over.

We kiss like we haven't seen each other in days, but we're running late and must come up for air. I help her into the car, and we're off again, my suit jacket swinging on a hanger behind me as I test the cornering ability of my Porsche on the curvy roads.

"I guess I'll see you at the arena. Well, I'll see you, you won't see me," she says, but little does she know I always look for her.

"I'll see you. If we win, we can all celebrate together afterward."

"Okay, that works. I can sleep in tomorrow."

I marvel over how natural this feels, making plans together like we've known each other for years. It doesn't feel forced or awkward at all.

"Ditto, but the next game will be in Boston. Can you make it? Can you get off work?"

I don't want to beg and hope I don't sound sappy. But I'd be thrilled if she could make the game for me, not to check out the other team guys or work on their stats.

"Probably. I'll see what I can do."

We're moving fast in this newfound relationship. To say I'm nervous is an understatement. I'm taking risks with my crazy driving, and the same could be said about diving into this relationship so fast.

Callie asks, "So, do you always move this quickly with someone new?"

It's as if she can read my thoughts. I don't know how to answer and stall, adjusting the rear-view mirror, thinking of something to say. Honesty is the best policy, but people think I'm an ass when I share my opinion.

"I guess it depends. I can't vouch for every relationship I've been in, but sometimes it's best not to overthink things. I don't do complicated."

I drop her off at her house and toss the keys to her car before giving her a lingering kiss to remember me for the next few hours before jumping back in my vehicle. Waving goodbye, I drive to the arena, making it to the parking lot with a few minutes to spare. I get off being late to practice, but I can't do that shit in the playoffs. Besides, I can't risk not playing when I'm needed. And now is not the time to piss off the coach and be a deutsche to my teammates.

I hop out of my car, throw on my jacket, and see camera crews lined up outside our fence with their zoom lenses. I'd love to drop my pants and flash them my ass cheeks, but the public and my bosses would consider that inappropriate.

However, if we win the Stanley Cup, we can get away with more, claiming we were partying and don't remember anything. Worst case, we'll get a slap on the wrist, like a verbal warning not to repeat the bad behavior.

"Oh, my God, Zaney is here," Wyatt announces my entrance to the locker room. Most of the players clap, and Playoff Pete bends a knee.

"Fuck off." I can't help but grin as I make my way to my locker. I need to get moving to suit up.

"Oh, come on. We're not going to let you off that easy. You're almost late to a game you'd never risk missing, so what gives?" Bagel, AKA Kal, pokes.

"Callie," Wyatt answers for me.

"Oh jeez, are we losing another bachelor soon?" Kal needles me, but he gets up and follows me when I don't answer.

"Say it's not so," he says, shocked. His jaw is dropping faster than a puck.

"Hey, put your game face on and stop concerning yourself with the hot chicks I date."

"That's better." He chuckles and returns to warm up for the game by doing squats with no weights and stretching his legs.

The truth will come out later if we all go out. But for now, I need to focus on my A-game.

"How's it going with Callie?" Wyatt asks, keeping his voice low.

"Great, so much so, I don't recognize myself. It's moving fast, and I don't know if I can handle it. I've never had a woman I want to impress so much, y'know?"

"Yeah, tell me about it," he quips, slapping me on the shoulder.

"So, you ready?"

"Always. To be the rookie on the team and be in the playoffs, are you kidding me? And then we have my wedding, so make sure you keep your calendar clear."

"Oh, for sure, serious bachelor party, dude."

"That's what I'm talking about. There's the Alexandre we all know and love."

It suddenly occurs to me that maybe Wyatt thinks I've changed somehow. Is that how it happens? A pretty lady comes along, draws me in with her evident charm, and then the incredible sex seals the deal? Do I have a say in the matter, or will that only fuck up a good thing?

Callie is older than the girls I typically date, and like most women, I'm sure she's looking for a commitment. I'm not sure I want that, but I don't want to lose her while figuring things out. I might not be able to get her back if I fuck it up.

∽

We enter the tunnel, and the fanfare starts. My heart races from the energy drink and a whiff of smelling salts, nasty shit, but it gets us revved up.

I'll limit myself to one look at Callie in the stands to prove I'm not pussy whipped. Our team is announced, so we spring onto the ice like champions with a shot at the Cup.

20

CALLIE

Hmm, interesting. I can't tell if his hesitation to answer my tough questions is a sign that he cares enough to join me in the express lane . . . or a warning that he wants to get off at the next exit. I must be nuts to want a relationship with Alexandre after only knowing him for a week.

But the more I'm around him, the more I throw caution to the wind and common sense out the window. This is a risky proposition at best, but I decide to give him the benefit of the doubt.

Me, the queen of conservative moves. Resident loner. Men beware.

After a long kiss with the promise of more later, he tosses me the keys to my car, jumps in his Porsche, and tears out of my driveway. He's left himself no room for error because he picked me up, and now, he's on his way back to the arena for work.

I don't know why he went to all the effort. I could have asked Sarah or another co-worker for a ride. I told him he was silly to risk being late to the game because of me, but he wouldn't take 'No' for an answer.

It reminds me of the way he persisted until I agreed to go to lunch with him on what I like to think of as our first date. All the signs indicate that he's used to getting his way or likes to be in control.

Maybe a bit of both?

I can't fault him. I'm the same way, but it's different for jocks. My gut tells me that his good looks win most women over, and that's something I can't compete with.

Men with perfect bodies, like the marble statue *The David,* which pays homage to the male species, is uncommon, especially in this sparsely populated state. A handsome man around here is enough to make any woman swoon.

Growing up with no siblings to play with and my parents' constant bickering, I loved to read as an escape. One of my favorite books was *Gone with the Wind,* and Rhett Butler was the man of my dreams instead of the popular boy bands of the 90s. Alexandre may not be Rhett, but he's just as golden, in my opinion.

After Alexandre leaves, I realize I forgot to ask him if my car is fixed. I assume so, but I slide in and click the ignition key forward to make sure. I'm relieved when the car turns over.

He didn't let me down.

A man who can shoot a puck and fix a dead battery. That's worth a few bonus points on my scorecard.

I sigh; the points are adding up for this jock. He's proven himself to be honest and loyal. Two qualities I admire in a man. He's not the type I ever thought I'd date, but now I'm seeing sides of him the press doesn't report and getting to know the man he is when the cameras and spotlights are not around.

I texted Sarah that I had gotten home safely and would meet her at the arena in one hour. Leaving Lucy alone for another evening makes me feel guilty, so I mix brown rice in her food for a treat. I take her for a quick walk down the road, enjoying the shade of the tall red oaks and maple trees. Their leaves will change soon, and I look forward to the vibrant colors of fall.

I have my TV set to record my favorite show, *The Affair,* as it's the final season, and I want to see how it ends. The storyline jumped the shark and got weird the past two seasons, and I almost stopped watching. However, it's getting interesting again as the show ties up loose ends, and I can't wait to see if the two main characters will get back together.

After a quick shower, I dry off and pull on some skinny jeans. I wear a tank over my bra and pull on a Mauler's jersey over my head. The goalie's name, McDavid, is stitched on the back.

Satisfied with how I look in the full-length mirror, I sit on the edge of the bed and tug on my black suede boots to keep my feet warm.

I apply some makeup, but I'm tired, and nothing I use can fix that. It might be a coffee at the arena tonight instead of beer. Then again, knowing my boyfriend is out there playing, I'm sure to be wide awake and glued to the edge of my seat.

SARAH and I meet by the will call window and, with the oversized jersey she's wearing, I can't tell she's preggers because the shirts are all so big. Her belly isn't that big, but soon it will start to show in her work clothes.

"You're glowing. How are you feeling?" I ask, hugging her.

"Sick all the time. It's a weight loss plan, proven to keep me from gaining a pound during pregnancy."

"You okay?"

"So far."

"How is James taking it?"

"He's supportive, but I think it's out of guilt." The twinkle in her eye and the smirk on her lips tells me she's milking this at home. I can't say I blame her.

"Let's go get your mind off it," I suggest, swinging an arm over her shoulder.

"So, Alexandre took care of fixing my car."

"Wow, that is nice. How did he do that and still get his nap in before the game?"

"Don't know." I shrug and hope the man isn't too tired. It's not like either of us got much sleep last night by the time he twisted my body into every position known to the Kama Sutra and then some. Clearly, he's picked up a few tricks in his years of dating.

"And you look as tired as I feel."

"Yeah, I'm running on caffeine and adrenaline. What are we eating?"

"Healthy grilled chicken I guess, with fries, of course," she says, stepping up to the counter to order.

"And mayo," I chime in to remind her of my addiction to the white condiment. It's probably all fat, but eating extra-crispy fries tastes much better.

We eat standing at a high-top table before taking our sodas with us to find our seats. The seats are amazing, on the blue line and within shouting distance of the team.

I'm beginning to think he's trying to impress me. Or maybe he wants me to know where he can find me during the game. I have yet to catch him looking my way, but he admitted he could see me.

You can bet your last dollar I'll try to catch him at it.

Why am I constantly thinking about him? I catch myself off in la-la land, daydreaming about him and his cute smile when I should be working. I find myself checking out men during the day, comparing them to him—the horror of it.

"How long do you think Alexandre and I will last?"

"Girl, you can't go into a relationship and have it stamped with an expiration date. He's not a can of peaches, for Christ's sakes."

"You're right. I'm being ridiculous. I don't understand what he sees in me when he can have that." I point to the Jumbotron overhead as it zooms in on a cute cheerleader type sitting in the stands, looking like she stepped out of the Sports Illustrated swimsuit edition.

"If you compare yourself to everyone, you'll never keep a guy. Fake it until you make it."

"Yeah." I have no reason to be insecure, but life has taught me that when something is too good to be true, it usually is, and I'm just waiting for the mirage to disappear.

In just a few days, Alexandre has ruined all men for me. If we don't work out, I'm so screwed because there is no way I'm going to date some juiced-up jock I meet at the gym.

I'm addicted to Alexandre. I can't picture myself with anyone else. I must be falling in love with this arrogant jock whose only love has been hockey and himself.

"Do you think these guys are capable of settling down? Being faithful?"

"Time will tell, some are, and some have deals with their wives. Don't worry. Have fun." She puts her hand to her mouth and looks slightly green until her nausea passes.

"Pregnancy isn't a walk in the park, is it?"

"Rarely, but I'm kind of excited."

"Me too. I'll be Auntie Callie again. I can't wait to have one of my own."

"Be careful what you wish for. . ."

"I know, nothing too soon. Wait until you are married two years. Look at me. The chances of that are slim to none. I'm trying to be cool with Alexandre," I say the words and pretend my new relationship is casual, but my heart and body know better.

"Ha! Sure you are. If so, why are your eyes glued to him even when you talk to me?"

"Yeah, I can't help myself." I sigh, totally smitten with the man in a uniform. "He's ruined all men for me. I have a weakness for a hard body, a chiseled jawline, and a perfect nose," I jest. "Who knew?"

"Me." She gives me an impish smile, and I wrap my arm around her, giving her a half hug. "So, who got your ass back into life? Who picked you up after your breakup? This girl." She points to herself with her thumb.

"You had my back, I know. But we wouldn't be sitting here if I had dated sooner."

"Touché."

We're winning the game, and Playoff Pete is looking good, but I have a terrible feeling that he will be traded, and I hope it won't strain my relationship with Alexandre.

Who, I might add, is playing well and gets an assist, with Wyatt making the goal. Wyatt has turned out to be an excellent investment. Hockey is a game of speed nowadays, and the owners all want kids with fast legs and lots of depth.

Watching Alexandre from the stands, I hope we win so I can meet the team and celebrate later. I like him in my bed at night when we snuggle as we fall asleep. I've been without a man for so long that I can't tell if I'm overly attached to the man in my bed or am I just addicted to sex with him?

Even his enormous cock is perfect— and well-trained. I can't wait to get my hands on his firm buttocks again. I plan to enjoy this until it all blows up in my face because that's what usually happens. Any other ending is foreign to me.

"I'm going to grab another soda. Want one?"

"You have to ask? It's not like I can have a beer."

"Right." I leave her, but before I can grab the drinks, I get a text from our boss, Logan. He wants me to call him.

I don't understand why I must call him during a playoff game.

But I do it anyway.

"Hey, Callie, we are working on a deal and want to know if you agree that the numbers all point to us needing more defense and depth on the team."

"Yes, they do."

"Okay, just wanted to make sure."

"Is Peety being traded?"

"More than likely. We can get a one-year contract on a defenseman who won the Stanley Cup last year, and we think he'll be a game-changer. Not to mention, we can get a great forward with the money we save in salary."

"He's gone after the playoffs?"

"Yep," he says rather matter-of-fact. His indifference doesn't surprise me. It's wheeling and dealing. It's nothing new to any of us in the office, but it's personal now that I'm dating a player. And it's complicated because he's friends with Peety.

My heart sinks. Logan doesn't think we're going to make it this year. I can't deny it's a long shot. We almost missed qualifying for the playoffs because the leading scorer was out with a lower-body injury, making it a difficult season. We have a weak defensive team, and our specialty teams didn't pick up until late in the season. Even at that, I'm surprised we made it this far because it was a long shot.

This puts a damper on my evening, but I can't let on to Sarah and Alexandre that I know what will happen after the race for the Cup.

I return with two sodas, but I can't relax. My nervous twitch has my right leg bouncing up and down like a jackhammer.

"What's wrong?"

"Nothing," I lie.

I can't stop fidgeting and am now chewing through the ice in my cup. How long can I hide this from Peety? Do I tell Alexandre? How is the team going to react? How will Alexandre react when he finds out? What will be the reaction in the locker room?

In retrospect, caffeinated soda was a poor choice. I should have ordered vodka and cranberry instead—and made it a double.

"What's the matter with you, Callie? I thought we were going to relax."

Feeling like I'm ready to explode from the anxiety, I let out a groan.

"Well, I have to tell someone, or I'll lose it. I can't take the stress."

"What?" She peers at me intently and leans toward me, anticipating the worst.

"It's official, Pete's up for a trade as soon as the playoffs are over. And Alexandre got wind of it from some reporter last week, so he came to my office. We're keeping this a secret from the team. We have to." I shrug.

"So, you're between a rock and a hard spot."

"Yes, and now we're involved, as in involved."

"Will it be okay?"

"I don't know. I'm sure he suspects it's likely to happen, but thinking about it and reality are two different things. I should know."

"Ugg, I hate this secret shit. But it's out of our hands."

"Of course it is. But if we win, we're all going out tonight, and I don't know how I'm going to face the guys."

"Oh boy, I see your dilemma."

"And on top of that, Alexandre is a great guy."

"That's so sweet," she coos.

"I know. Fucking adorable. He's earning so many points on my long checklist it's scaring the shit out of me."

"Yeah, I can't tell if moving fast is good or not. But either way, you'll find out soon enough."

It's nice that Sarah can re-affirm my rational thoughts.

"Not knowing the outcome of the trade and this relationship has me tied up in knots." I consciously start biting my fingernails.

Damn, damn, and double damn.

I kicked this habit before, and my nerves have brought it back. I can't go back to biting my nails like a kid. What would Alexandre think? And all those hot models lurking around the guys all the time?

"Relax, don't read so much into it. I'm sure it will all work out."

"Says the woman with an unplanned baby number four. . ." I tease.

"I know, but all things considered, you're living the life right now. Fucking enjoy. Before long, you might have little rug rats running around, and then you will complain about how bored you are and tired and that you have no social life. Take it from me. Have the time of your life now."

Her practical advice talks me down from the ledge.

"I love you."

"I know, I love you too; now let's watch the guys."

"I know. I'm so discombobulated with this."

"It happens to the best of us, sweetie. Just think about your crush on number twenty-three and how he's rocking your world."

"He's rocking something all right."

We're in the second period, and we're up by one. I yell when Alexandre has the puck, and he puts one in the net. My voice is raspy from screaming like a fanatic.

"Down girl," Sarah teases me.

She leaves before the game ends to beat the traffic out of the arena, and we've got the game in the bag. We're up by two and only two minutes left in the game when a player makes a top-shelf goal, sealing the deal for us as we kill the clock. Our team leaves the ice happy but takes the win lightly.

The Sharks could have made two quick goals in the last two minutes, but it's been an uphill battle for them tonight. However, my 'Spidey sense' tells me that our luck is about to change when we leave town in two days.

I leave the arena and head to the Camden Hills Brewing Company to reserve a large area for the guys. From what I gather, I have an hour's wait while they do some ritual with a shower, beer, and horseplay.

I order a drink and nurse it. I could trust Alexandre with the news, but it would serve no purpose. Right now, the team needs to be focused on winning.

The guys make a raucous entrance into the pub, and the fans light up, cheering and congratulating them as they pass by.

Alexandre's scent washes over me as he pulls up a chair, and the table quickly fills with pitchers of beer bought by patrons.

The door to the pub never seems to close for long as the rest of the team piles in with their wives, girlfriends, and random puck bunnies. The noise, the loud voices, it all overwhelms me. It's like eating an edible of wonky stuff and pushing me over with anxiety that makes me nauseous and dizzy.

Everyone is trying to be heard over the big screen TV showing the game highlights. The announcer recaps it with the players they interviewed and then cuts to another game on the West Coast.

Alexandre gives me a quick kiss before heading to the bar to buy a round of shots for the guys. I turn to watch him walk away and try not to get jealous when some chicks approach him, wanting autographs and selfies with him. He gives into the demands for a group shot, and I swear one of them is hitting on my guy. I see red, even though I'm not the jealous type.

He's going home with me. Why do I care? I have nothing to be insecure about.

And yet, he lets the girls put their arms around him, and he smiles like he enjoys it.

Ah, the man in public is different than the man in private. Or is he?

He's acting like a stereotypical callous jock, and I feel invisible. I want to leave, but my feet are firmly planted on the chair as I patiently wait more than twenty minutes for him to return. The best outcome for me for staying is that I'm feeling better.

"Think you've had enough adoration for the night?"

"Oh, me? That's nothing." He pounds his beer, and hoists his shot, and the team cheers and tosses it back.

He's not acting like it's anything, and maybe it's not. I dismiss it and turn to talk with Wyatt and Emily. I liked getting to know her a little at the last game, and they make a cute couple.

"I can't have you wearing another player's jersey," Alexandre whispers in my ear.

"Why?"

"Because you're my girl."

I melt.

Playoff Pete is the life of the party, replaying minutes of the game, and I wish I could crawl under the table with the secret I have to carry.

21

———

ALEXANDRE

The game was exhausting, as we knew it would be, but times that by one hundred. My legs are shredded, and Peety hands out some bananas after the game. We shower, give each other smack, relive the game's highlights, and curse the refs for their shitty job, but we have two wins, and it's on to Boston.

We live to play another day and worry about that game when it gets here. One thing athletes know is that we have to put the loss behind us. We can't let it mess with our heads, and we can't worry about what lies ahead until it's time.

I hurry to get cleaned up and dressed as I'm anxious to meet up with Callie. Wyatt and I arrive at the bar first and find her sitting with Emily. Callie is wearing the goalie's jersey, which is cool, but she needs to be wearing mine, so I make a mental note to have one made, that way, she has a choice. For all I know, we'll crash and burn as a couple, and she will burn it in effigy.

She smiles up at me as I bend to kiss her. My hair is still damp from the shower, but I smell better than I did in the locker room after the game. A dumpster full of rotting food smells better than the combined odor of sweaty bodies, jerseys, skates, and pads. It quite literally takes one's breath away, it's that powerful.

Callie unwraps her arms from my neck, and I head to the bar to get some shots for the table. Two puck bunnies come up to me and introduce themselves, totally crushing on me, and like a puppy, I love the attention. Who wouldn't, right? Then they want pictures, and I find it hard to tear myself away as they keep asking questions and time passes until finally, I end up telling them I need to get back to my friends and leave.

It happens all the time, and I go with it because it's better than saying no from the get-go, which I've done and pissed off too many fans over the years with my abruptness.

But my new girl, well, she makes me want to be a better person, so I make nice with the girls until I catch her looking at me with a perplexed look.

Shit, I fucked up. Maybe I enjoyed it too much and for too long.

Maybe she needs more attention, and I need to be more of a dick to strangers, that way, people will leave me alone.

I bring Callie a beer along with mine, and a server follows behind me with a tray full of tequila shots for the table. Whereby we each lift a shot glass.

"To the best fucking team ever. Stanley Cup or bust," I make a toast, and we all clink our shot glasses and toss it back. There are twelve of us tonight, and Luc orders another round.

This is all well and good, but there is no way I'm risking whiskey dick tonight, so I drink a few beers and pace myself. But the shots keep coming, and I decide we need to get out of here.

I look for Callie and spot her talking to Wyatt and Emily. I watch as Peety stops by their table and introduces himself. It's hard to tell from this distance, but Callie looks pale.

Fuck, this isn't good. She's not one to hide her feelings well. In fact, they usually pour out with little encouragement. I haven't known her long, but this much I know to be true.

It's encouraging when I see her smile and chat with him. She's congratulating him on the win when I join them at the table.

Time to boo-boo.

I follow Callie to her place, and whatever bothered her before seems to have passed, so I decide not to bring it up. Not sure if that's for my protection or hers.

After we take care of Lucy, we race upstairs for fun under the sheets, and it's another round of games, the ones I like just as much as hockey.

I wake up to the sound of Lucy's collar making a tinkling sound from her dog tags hitting each other as she runs around the room. Callie is with her and bends over to kiss me.

"Morning, sleepy head, it's late."

"How late is it?"

"Not bad, ten."

"Oh, wow, sorry I slept so long."

"No problem. It's Saturday, but I have no clue what schedule you're on."

"One of hockey and you," I tease, grabbing her by her waist and pulling her back into bed. She's still wearing a cute two-piece nighty, implying the morning isn't over yet.

She squeals as she rolls over me, and I roll up on top of her and rub my growing beard over her face. It's scratchy, and she pushes me away.

"Stop." She giggles, but I don't listen.

"Say, Uncle." I nibble her neck.

"Never."

I give her a face wash, rubbing my hand down her face like she's one of the guys.

"Uncle!"

"That's more like it."

We make love, and each time we're together, it's better than the last. The ribbing I get from the guys for knowing her name has died down, and I wonder if they are right. Maybe saying your girlfriend's name does make a man fall in love.

I'm content to enjoy a lazy weekend recouping before we fly to Boston.

WE ARRIVE in Boston with a big splash. The press swarms our coach and the paparazzi snap pictures of us walking across the tarmac. I'm not surprised. Tonight is a big night, and the Sharks have home-ice advantage.

Callie got Monday off from work, so she can join me later. I bought her a plane ticket and reserved her a suite at the same hotel on the same floor. I'll need to stay in my room with a teammate, but that's okay. I'm happy she's willing to make the sacrifices to be with me, but I wonder how long it will last. Normally, it gets old for most girlfriends after a few months, and they stop coming around.

We arrive early, have a team meeting and then we fuck around the hotel and go out to lunch in groups before I return to meet her in the hotel lobby.

"What the fuck!" Someone is shouting, and I know that voice.

It's Playoff Pete, and he's in Callie's face. "I know who you are, and you're responsible for getting me traded after this run at the Cup." He's fired up and probably had a few too many at lunch, which isn't cool since tonight's game is critical.

"What do you mean?" I try to calm him down as strangers are looking at us.

"You're with management, and you knew I was being traded weeks ago." His finger is in Callie's face, and she's calm, but I'm ready to deck him.

"Look, cool down. Let's go somewhere and sort this out."

"No, and you're dating her. There's no way you didn't hear about it. Nice teamwork, Alexandre. You're a piece of shit."

Peety storms off, but he doesn't have a car, so we're good on that front.

I turn to Callie. "Is it true?"

"Yes, I wanted to tell you, but I didn't want to ruin your chance at the Cup because I knew it would throw your game off."

I'm sure her intentions were good, but I'm disappointed. "I thought we were a team. I know you have trust issues, but this is me, not Mitch. You could have told me."

"I'm stuck in the middle, Alexandre. If I tell you I'm violating my contract, if I don't, I'm a traitor in your eyes. There's nothing I could do." She shrugs her shoulders. She's right.

I get that. Obviously, I just thought I meant more to her, and I'm perturbed. This is our first argument, and the timing sucks. The added bummer is that it's over work-related bullshit.

Players and management don't mix, but I deluded into thinking we could make it work.

"I can't do anything about the trade. I don't make the final decisions. All I do is process and present the information."

"Yeah, useless information."

"In your opinion."

"Yeah, but it should be your opinion too." I storm off.

I'm a dick, I didn't know this would be so complicated. I don't function well with messy. I like to know what to expect when to expect it, and have a plan ready. There is no plan for this.

Callie goes to check in at the front desk while I comb through the hotel looking for Peety and come up empty. He might be by the poolside bar; the last thing he needs is more alcohol.

Sure enough, I find him there acting like an ass, bitching to the bartender about our team, which is something management won't forgive.

I rescue him from himself. I can relate to what it's like to be traded, but in truth, he had to know he wasn't an integral part of the team. He's getting older. I'll be there myself one day.

"Pete." I use a stern tone as I take him by the elbow.

"What, get away, you're an ass."

I hiss in his ear, "Look, you are making this difficult for yourself. Stop. I'll take you to your room."

He thinks briefly before sliding off the barstool and following me to the players' corridor.

"You knew. I thought you were my friend."

"I am, I was in a pickle myself, and I didn't know it was final until now. It's not Callie's fault. It's not her call. She runs the numbers, that's all."

"Someone at the pub recognized her and knew what she did for the company. There was a rumor floating around, and when none of my calls to management were returned, I figured it was a done deal."

I take his key card and get him in his room. "Look, you need to sober up, take a nap. We have a game tonight. You have a job to do. We need you."

"Sure you do, like a hangover." He flops face down on the bed.

I take his shoes off, put a blanket over him, and turn the air-conditioning low so he'll sleep better.

I swear we all have a bit of ice in our veins to play this game, and we're comfortable in the cold.

He mumbles something incoherent as I pick up the phone and leave a wake-up call for him so he won't be late.

Meanwhile, I'm torn on Callie. It's our first disagreement, and I have to get sleep before the game.

I head to my room, close the curtains, and make the room cooler before shucking my clothes, downing an eight-ounce bottle of water, and crawling under the covers, setting the alarm on the Tissot watch I wear on road trips.

I'm superstitious about where and when I wear my favorite watches. One watch for home games, one for away, and anything goes on days off. That is pretty much how I live my bachelor life.

I try to shake thoughts of Callie as I drift to sleep. My eye is on the prize, and that's the Stanley Cup.

I MAKE sure Peety is with us as we pile into the van to the arena. We're dressed to impress and walk with our chins up, but he should be ashamed of his immature behavior earlier.

I should have chosen him over Callie, but I couldn't do that, just like she couldn't choose between me and her career.

This is not the way I wanted this to go down at all. The guys give me weird looks in the locker room. They've all heard by now that I'm seeing the girl who they think is responsible for putting Peety on the chopping block.

The first time I stuck my neck out for someone, and this is what I get.

Hmm.

Well, lesson learned. I guess it's time to go back to being a glorious bastard.

WE FELT it going onto the ice. Our passing was off. Our defense fell, and the Sharks played like there was blood in the water. We couldn't get a puck in the net if our life depended on it.

Fuck, our chances at winning here are zero to none with this attitude, and I know better than to be the cheerleader for the team because that's just not me.

I don't give pep talks. It's up to the captain to boost morale and convince us that we can win tonight. But we all know that our heads aren't in it, and this just sucks.

"Great going, guys, what a way to fuck with our heads," someone mutters as he walks by. I don't care to look up to see who it is. The entire team is at odds with each other.

The fact is this is our reality. It could have been anyone on the team getting traded. This is the shitty part of professional hockey that we don't share with the public. When it comes to trading day, we put on a brave face, the team throws up a cute family picture on social media as a farewell, and we're on the next plane out. Literally. The wife packs if it's during the season because we don't have time.

A long season can feel like a meat grinder between all the back-to-back road trips. Plenty of guys come home to cranky wives and girlfriends, pressuring them for that engagement ring. Then, shortly after the season is over, the divorces and breakups start.

I'm in no hurry to go down that path. I come home to a quiet house, and when the nagging starts, I hit the road.

Players without a contract can go at any time, even with a contract, 'stuff' occurs.

I'm upset with the way things went down today but, like Callie, I'm stuck too. If I'm seen with her, it's not going to go down well. It will be even worse if the wives and girlfriends, aka WAGS, get ahold of her.

Maybe Callie can form an alliance with Emily, who doesn't hang out with the mean girls on the squad, choosing instead the women who aren't spreading gossip and fueling petty jealousies.

Some of the WAGS pick more catfights than any player on the ice looking to draw a penalty. I've avoided introducing her to them because they act like privileged private school teenagers filled with insecurities larger than their purses.

Maybe it's good this happened now before I fall in love.

The game ends, the locker room feels like a funeral home, and we drag our whipped asses back to the busses for a somber ride to the hotel.

Callie texts.

Sorry that we lost.

I'm not in a good mood.

She texts that she's watching the ending episode of her favorite show *The Affair,* and the last thing I want to do is hear about the ending with a dance sequence that sounds corny.

We're here until our game two nights from now, so I'll see her tomorrow. The problem is, I can't figure out what to do about the team or us.

22

CALLIE

It's soul-crushing that I know a player's fate before him. Up until this point, trades were just business and nothing personal. Getting to know the players and putting a face to their number brings them to life. But it also makes my job that much harder.

It's safe behind a desk. It's safe not dating. But I need to take more chances even if the female fans are overzealous with my guy.

Alexandre doesn't say much when I text him, and he doesn't call to talk. I don't know what to make of it, but I resist the urge to panic. I can understand him wanting to be alone after a loss. I'd probably feel the same way.

The loss tonight came as no surprise to the sportscasters. Before the game even started, they predicted that the Maulers wouldn't do well away from home. They blamed it on being away from home and the lack of home ice advantage.

I watch my show and get a restless sleep, wondering what the future holds. I'm not immersed in his life and nervous about living life in the public eye.

THE FOLLOWING DAY, I ran into Peety at the team's breakfast.

Towering over me at the coffee station, he leans in and says, "Hey, sorry about yesterday. I was a jerk. I'm under a lot of pressure, and it's tough knowing I'll be leaving."

I can't be angry with someone so sweet, and the realization is that even though he's a star, he's human, and even athletes have bad days.

"Don't worry about it. How's Alexandre?"

"Probably not too happy about the loss."

"Yeah, well . . . you guys will win the next one." I try to give him some hope.

I haven't heard from Alexandre, and he hasn't answered any of my texts. Maybe he's not up yet.

Great. I'm in Boston alone, with a team that's eating its own, and my boyfriend is MIA.

He can have it if this is what it's like to be his girlfriend.

I call Sarah.

"What's wrong?"

Damn, she's good. She reads through me like I'm tracing paper.

"Alexandre is in some funk and acting weird. I don't know if this is going to work."

"Look, there's going to be ups and downs in a relationship, and this is a stressful time for both of you, but mostly him."

"The news of Peety broke."

"The agents were calling earlier. It's been busy here. I figured that might be happening. Then there is the ever-present gossip around the coffee pot."

"Yeah, I hear 'you. Nothing is a secret. How are you doing?"

"Great, when I'm not eating." She chuckles.

"Hmm. Well, we'll talk about that when I get back. The team flies back tomorrow after the game, and I fly out the following morning."

"That sucks."

"Yeah, but breaking the rules isn't good either. I doubt the team wants me on the plane with them anyway."

I'm hard on myself even though I can't change what transpired.

"Well, take it easy on the boys. Remember, they're adults. They'll get over it."

"I'm not so sure. I mean, you're right. I wish I knew how long that will take."

ALEXANDRE and I meet up for dinner, and the atmosphere is tense at best. He's not talking, and I don't know what to say. We go through the motions and somehow, we make conversation that is too polite.

As soon as we finish and walk out, a white van with the local sports station's colorful logo pulls up, and we're blinded by bright lights. Instinctively, I slip my arm through Alexandre's and look up at him for a cue on what to do.

His face remains stoic as he walks past the reporters without comment, ignoring their microphones and questions about the loss to the Sharks and the probability of Peety being traded.

We get into a cab and return to the hotel where we hang out in the sports bar. I pray to God that no one from the team comes in. My heart is racing, and it's not from caffeine. Or Alexandre.

Anxiety, pressure to fit in. Do I want to fit in? Am I special to Alexandre? I focus on the big screen TVs and take in the other hockey games going on tonight in other divisions, and I'm relieved when the sportscasters make no mention of last night's loss. A loss that puts more pressure on a win tomorrow.

Trying to be a good girlfriend during the worst period of a man's life leaves me outside my comfort zone. How do we bridge the chasm between us that feels wider than the Grand Canyon?

But I need to try. I don't want to fail at another relationship. I don't want to be shut out, yet I don't know how to help the situation.

"Is there anything I can do to make you feel better?"

"No."

His one-word answer is not what I wanted to hear, but it's gonna take more than that to scare me off.

"Well, Pete apologized to me this morning. I forgot to mention it. He says he was a bit drunk and upset, and he took it out on me."

"That's true. In hindsight, not as big of a deal as I made it out to be," he orders a beer. "What are you drinking?"

"Red wine, please."

He orders and charges it to his room.

"Well then, why did you storm into my office? And go through the charade of caring if you've always been resolved to it?"

"Normally, I don't get involved, but this felt like a fight worth fighting. Maybe I was trying to feel something, to make a difference, be a team player."

"I thought you were."

"The rumors are true, I show up late, I don't give my sticks away to kids after the games, and I'm not that personable with the reporters. I just 'show up so I don't get fined.'"

"What does that mean?" I sip the drink in front of me as I wait.

"It's a phrase that football players use when they have to talk to the press because if they don't, they will be fined. Well, hockey doesn't do that, but we do have obligations, but I do as little as possible." He takes another sip of his beer before turning his head to look me dead in the eye.

My heart skips a beat. The anticipation is building. Where is this going?

"Everything they say about me being rude and detached is true." He takes a few more sips of his frothy beer from his cold mug.

"So, why now? Why change?"

"Maybe the girls I dated were right when they said I have a heart as hard and black as a hockey puck. The more I walled myself off, the bigger the darkness inside me grew until one day it took over." He shrugs. "It was finally time to come out from behind the wall and do something for someone other than myself, y'know?"

"Yeah, I get it." I think that's me when I stay in instead of going out with co-workers and kayaking rather of going on a blind date. We make choices that might not be in our best interest in the long run because we're doing what we want instead of what might be best for ourselves.

I'm glad he's opening up to me, but there's no room to celebrate with this cloud of disappointment looming over us. I want to cheer him up or comfort him in some way, but I can't. I don't know how. As Sarah says, they're men. They'll figure their shit out; it's what they do.

I'm surprised that he opened up as much as he did as he's usually not that forthcoming, and take this as a sign that his mood is from the game and not directly affected by me.

We finish our drinks and call it a night.

On the way to our rooms, I glance at him to check his demeanor, looking for signs that he's still into me, however, his face remains expressionless.

Fuck, this can't be good.

We arrive at my room. He stops long enough to lightly kiss my lips. "Have a good night, Callie." Then he turns on the heels of his expensive dress shoes and leaves me wondering what the hell just happened.

It's unrealistic to expect the team to sweep the series, and I knew it was only a matter of time before we would lose a game. I mean, it's the most competitive part of the year, but I've never felt so unprepared for anything more than I do now. I need to stop feeling like I must make him happy and fix everything. But that's not my job.

Alone in my room, I kick off my heels, flop on the bed and turn on the TV to keep me company. Somewhere during the night, I wake up to the sound of the same show replaying, and I turn it off, hoping I can get some sleep. I'm a bit ragged from the tension with my boyfriend.

Daylight breaks and I'm still in my clothes from last night. I wish I was home, but it'd be rude to leave before the final game on this road trip. To say that I'm a hindrance is an understatement.

I text Sarah, who's at work.

Hang in there. Let it go, try not to overreact.

I don't know if we'll get back to where we were.

No one ever does. If it's meant to be, it will. If not, there will be others.

Ugg, that's not what I wanted to hear. She's trying to cheer me up, but what if Alexandre and I are only a passing flame that have already burned out?

Relationships take time. You have ups and downs; you're just going through a rough patch. Man up, girl.

She's right. I have to grow some thick skin if I want to date a professional athlete. But can I do this? Doubtful. In retrospect, I've never been a cheerleader, and Mitch wasn't that good at it, either.

I'm doomed to fail. Always a bridesmaid and never a bride? Hell, I don't even have a single girlfriend, and I've only been a bridesmaid once, and she was my cousin.

Alexandre texts me to meet him for breakfast.

I wait a minute before acknowledging him. I don't want to appear over-excited.

Meanwhile, I throw the bedsheets off me and spring from bed, wondering what to wear.

I don't want to take too long, so I grab a pair of jeans and a cute white top and apply a sparse amount of makeup to cover my tired face.

Grabbing my room key, I meet the team for their breakfast in a roped-off section of the dining area.

Alexander greets me with a smile as if nothing is amiss. He gives me a warm kiss, and I've forgotten that I've died a thousand deaths waiting for it. I find solace in his display of affection in public.

And it's the least he can do after I spent yesterday on the outside looking in on a team struggling on many levels.

Then it hits me that they've been experiencing ups and downs the entire season. They are resilient. They aren't children looking for validation from a parent. They support each other because they are a team. I'm the newbie. I'm the one who needs to learn how to cope with their ups and downs and the occasional empty bed.

Mostly the empty bed, and maybe that's why I'm a bit off. I like his arms around me and wish we could hole up together. Our timing is off and on with us. However, Alexandre is a seasoned player. I'm the rookie.

I take the plate he hands me and pretend this is normal and it's just another day. We find a place to sit, and he returns for coffee, walking with his head up and shoulders back. The team has hit the reset button.

When he returns, our eyes meet, and I smile because seeing him walking toward me makes me happy. Like the first date, the spark is back, and we lean across the table and lock lips in a long kiss that electrifies my body.

God damn, I still want him.

"So, what did you do the other day?"

"Just some sightseeing, normal tourist stuff."

"If I know you, I'd guess a museum." He digs into his big breakfast.

"Well, I went to the Aquarium." I chuckle.

"No kidding. How was it?"

And it's as if the last twenty-four hours never happened as we settle into a conversation and eat together like we've been doing this routine forever.

Maybe Sarah is right. Perhaps it will all work out despite my inner turmoil that a guy like him would choose me.

23

ALEXANDRE

The next day, we're still not ourselves and suffer a second loss to the Sharks.

The Boston arena is a tough place to win a game. The crowd is deafening, and we can't hear each other on the ice. The Sharks wear us down, having us skate up and down the ice as if we're in a speed skating competition instead of hockey. We never get close enough to the net to score, and the game ends in a shutout. Now we're in the crapper.

We go straight from the locker room to the airport so I'm not able to see Callie after the game. It's probably for the best because I'm in a foul mood. The flight home is always so much longer after a loss. Thankfully, we're on a private charter with top-shelf liquor and gourmet food to distract ourselves. Most of the guys are on their phones or talking to each other about anything other than the game. Some have their seats in full recline to watch movies or listen to music.

It's not the same as a win when everyone is still jacked up on the adrenaline rush. The coaches are watching footage of the game, dissecting every replay to see what we could have done differently.

There will be a team meeting tomorrow to review the changes we must make.

Callie is in an unfortunate position where her career doesn't align with mine. Some would consider it a conflict of interest because she's with the same company and she's viewed as a member of management. No matter what, it's the hat she wears, and she can't change it. She's just doing her job, and it's not her fault that someone is being traded.

Peety and I could have handled the bad news much better, and we should have, seeing as how we've been around long enough to know this is how the franchises operate. We've all come to accept that we'll lose at least one or more teammates after a run at the Cup. Management is always trying to improve aspects of the team they consider weak. Their decisions may not be personal, but we're all still human and have feelings.

After we land, we go our separate ways, some guys hop in their sports cars they can drive during the warm months, some getting picked up by their women. My girl is still in Boston waiting for a flight home tomorrow. It's after midnight, and I'm beat.

I let myself in my house and text Callie I'm home and will pick her up at the airport tomorrow.

I don't hear back and assume she fell asleep. She looked tired, and I hope she can get some rest. Eerily, the house is quiet, too quiet. Instead of it feeling like my safe haven, I'm longing for the day Callie and I will live together.

I wish she were here. I'm missing her cute laugh, and the way she walks into a room like she's gliding on ice without need for skates. Nothing about her makes me think she's after me for the fame or the fortune.

For the first time, I miss a girl. Just the sight of her at my game warms my heart. Instinctively, I know this is more than some infatuation. The girls I passed on before were immature, paying more attention to their phone or their Instagram followers than they did to me. This time, I have someone genuine. Someone who will come to my games to see me play, not for the photo op or social media post. She's the first girl who has my best interest at heart.

What does she see in me? I don't know. She's too good for me, and I don't deserve her, but it doesn't keep me from wanting her.

I fall into bed, where I toss and turn, unable to sleep. I blame it on the stress from the loss and telling myself the house is too warm. But in my dark heart, I miss her body next to mine, and the fact of the matter is, we touch toes under the cool bedsheets all night long. We've grown close in our short time together; if we were together tonight we'd be wrapping our bodies around each other like a Twizzler.

I roll over to grab my phone from the nightstand and recheck my messages to see if she texted. Nothing.

I eventually fall into a restless sleep, but when I wake up in the morning, I'm just as tired as I was yesterday.

I WALK into the airport and when I meet Callie, I immediately pull her into me, inhale deeply, and bury my face in her hair. With my huge arms around her, holding her tight, I'm happy she's home, safe and sound. I never want to let her go.

"Hi, babe." I give her a quick kiss on her cheek and neck.

"Hey."

Her tone is flat instead of bubbly, and I wonder if the past few days were too much for her. She still has her 'dating a hockey player' training wheels on, and she has yet to deal with the constant public scrutiny and the team riff.

"You okay?" I ask, hoping she's just tired.

"Oh, yeah." The inflection in her voice convinces me she's okay.

"Really?" I grab her carry-on bag, wrap my arm around her shoulders, and walk to the parking lot.

It's a short walk because this airport is small enough to fit into the parking lot of most international airports. This area is so rural, and our population is so small, there's no reason to have a larger one.

"I'm just tired. That's all. Some of us don't get to fly private," she teases.

"Whoa, well, fine. If you want to give up carbs and train daily, then be my guest."

"Umm," she pretends to consider it a second, "nope. Can't do that. I like my grilled hotdogs too much, and I doubt those are on your trainer's menu."

"You're right unless they're made of tofu!"

She giggles. I kiss her on the forehead.

"How about lunch, and I'll take you home?"

"Sure."

"I'm sorry about the drama on the road. It was stupid, and unprofessional at best, and none of it was your fault. I just thought I could get you to change your mind about Peety."

"I told you it's not up to me, and to present anything other than the truth to my boss would be unethical."

"Oh, I know." I let her in the passenger side of my little red Roadster.

I slide behind the wheel and start the car.

"How were you going to change my mind?"

"Little Ms. Inquisitive, are you?"

"Yes, tell me."

"I just thought I'd be able to charm your pants off and save Peety in the process."

"Hmm. You did. Did you?"

"What, is there a law against it?"

"No."

"What?"

"What? I asked first," she argues.

"Can we just forget it? It's been a long day, and I didn't get much sleep."

"No, we can't forget it. I can't believe you put on this entire, elaborate," her voice raises, "charade to get me to do what you want. You are such an arrogant ass."

"What? It's not like that." I try to explain, but the way she's glaring at me tells even the most clueless man to shut the fuck up. I return to the road even though I'm miffed and would normally argue more with anyone else.

"Take me home."

"Callie, it's not like that." But the look on her face tells me she's not in the mood to listen.

The ride to her house is one of the most uncomfortable rides of my life, and I'm stuck. Nothing will change her mind while she's in this mood, and I don't want to make it worse.

If I could get her to calm down, and she'll realize it's not as it seems. She does have a right to be mad because I asked her out under false pretenses. Initially, I thought she would be hypnotized by my charm and go to bat for me, but in the process...

I fell for her.

How did I not see this before? The sweet cuddles, the sexy late-night texts, the fact of the matter—I can't stop thinking about her.

It has all the earmarks of a relationship. We laugh, we argue, but at the end of the day . . . . we're still the same people who started it together. There's nothing fake about her, no fake eyelashes, nails, or personality.

No, Callie surprises me in the most remarkable ways. She's supportive and patient even when I'm in my world and not sharing the moment with her.

She gets me, and we love the same things, hockey, dogs, and Maine.

In Maine, we have this thing called Newman Day, named after a

Paul Newman movie. The Maniacs at Longfellow University lifted a line from one of his movies and turned it into a beer-drinking challenge. Every year, on the twenty-fourth of April, the students drink twenty-four beers in 24 hours. No joke, true story.

The rest of the year, we have a crazy radio personality called the Hillbilly Weatherman. He cracks me up whenever he opens his mouth to give a weather report, using colorful commentary to describe how cold it will be.

I stop in front of her house. "Can we at least talk about this?"

"Nope." She gets out, grabs her bag from the backseat, and, without looking back, stomps off to her house.

Did Callie just break up with me?

24

———————

CALLIE

Well, this takes the cake. I should have known it was just a matter of time before Alexandre Holloway showed his true colors.

What an arrogant bastard to think I would compromise my integrity for him. I have such a sour taste in my mouth I think I might throw up.

When he took me to lunch after the phone call with Mitch, he was such a great listener and seemed to be so concerned when, all the while, he was using me to get what he wanted—well played. I feel like such an idiot.

He knew I was vulnerable, and he took advantage of me.

Now, I wonder, is there anything he said or did that was genuine?

My only satisfaction is that he didn't get me to compromise myself.

But I fell for it. Or rather, him.

I close the door behind me, drop my bag, and sink to the floor, gathering Lucy into my welcoming arms. God, I love this dog. She's my everything.

"I missed you, girl. I'm so glad you don't have a boyfriend. I don't know how we would get through it."

Maybe I should cut myself some slack. To not fall for Alexandre's hard body and charm is like . . . well, it's like passing on the juiciest and tastiest Angus beef burger ever made. He's hard to resist, and I'm sure I'm not his first casualty. There's probably a long line of broken hearts before me.

He should consider going into sales if his hockey career doesn't work out. I never met a man so cold and calculating . . . and charming at the same time. I kick myself for not being a better judge of character.

My phone plays a cute ringtone from my favorite show, *The Whole of the Moon*. This means one thing. Alexandre is calling.

I feel bad about not answering his call and let it go to voicemail.

To distract myself, I play with Lucy, getting her riled up and roughhousing with her, trying to make up for not being home for two days. I missed her.

After showering to get the road dirt off, I text Sarah that I'm home.

I yawn and question why I'm so exhausted. I didn't do much of anything. I chalk it up to drama with the team and a broken heart.

I can't imagine working this out with Alexandre. His motives are a betrayal at best, and I won't tolerate that, even if he is the hottest piece of ass ever to share my bed.

It will be a while before I can erase the memory of the steamy nights we shared, how I writhed and twisted under his unrelenting kisses and tongue licking. Or how only the slightest touch of his hand on my naked body makes my skin break out in goosebumps.

I couldn't resist him. He's one of those guys you have to try just once. But once can be devastating. And to think we were supposed to be together, we talked, he promised, and now I'm collateral damage.

I ignore the texts blowing up my phone and throw a frozen

dinner into the microwave. I fill Lucy's food bowl while I wait for the timer to ding.

Using hot pads, I carry my meal to the counter and sink into a kitchen barstool to eat the sad, reminding me I'm single again. And alone.

Lonely. I remember the tell-tale signs of loneliness, and it's now hitting me like a Tsunami. *Whoosh.*

Curiosity gets the best of me while I wait for my food to cool down, and I pick up my phone and start reading his messages.

He says he didn't mean it, and we need to talk.

Is he pleading with me?

Is he serious?

Hmm.

It's Wednesday, and Sarah will be at work. I give her a call.

She answers, "Girl, the mood here is the worst. There's talk that the guys are up shit's creek."

"Hmm, well, yeah. We got clobbered in Boston."

"You can say that again."

I hear Logan barking orders in the background like a pit trader on Wall Street.

"I gotta go. You're in tomorrow, aren't you?"

"Yeah, call me later," I add quickly.

"Okay, bye."

I get more texts. Alexandre has two tickets for me to game 5. I don't even know why he's spending the money. Surely, he can find better things to do. My chest wells up with emotions. These emotions are like silly strings out of a can. Only they're not silly. My thoughts are all over the place as I finish eating and dump the container in the trash can.

Instead of Rocky Road ice cream, I pick up my carry-on bag and head upstairs to change into sweats before curling up in bed with Lucy next to me.

I get a bit weepy and need a distraction, so I turn the TV on to watch a previously recorded show. My eyelids grow heavy, and I drift off with my arms wrapped around Lucy.

The phone rings, and after glancing at my phone, I learn I've been asleep for hours. Sarah's calling me on her way home from work.

"What's up?"

"Major scrambling in the situation room." In other words, *management is freaking the fuck out.*

"I can only imagine. Glad I'm not there today. But when I return, I'll have plenty of work to do before the June trade deadline."

"Yes, but what's up with you? You sound like shit."

"Thanks."

"You know what I mean," she apologizes.

"Yeah, yeah. I don't know. I think Alexandre and I broke up. Or rather, I broke up with him."

"Oh, no, what happened?"

"Turns out he was only dating me to try and get me to say Peety needed to stay on the team. Though he could sweet talk me out of my panties, he did." I burst out crying and carrying on about the situation even though it must sound like gibberish.

"Hold on, you believe that?"

"Yeah, that's what he said. He's an asshole whether or not he admits it."

"Look, I can't read minds or futures. If I could, I'd have a maid and vacations in the tropics every winter. But maybe there's an explanation."

I can't contain my chuckle because it's my best friend and she's the only person in the world I trust for good judgment.

"He left us tickets to game 5," I murmur, groggy from sleep.

"See, that's a sign. You're not broken up. He's still making an effort. Maybe it's just a break. You two have moved fast, and it's a stressful time for both of you. You need a minute to regroup."

"Well, I'm done. Anything requiring this much work and having me on an emotional roller coaster isn't worth it," I reply, agitated. Love isn't supposed to make a person miserable.

"That's not true. It's a different world, but it doesn't have to change how you feel about each other."

"Well, it does."

"No changing your mind?"

"Nope." I sniffle, trying not to cry again.

Her advice makes me feel better, but it will be weird to show up to work tomorrow.

"You are stubborn. I'll give you that. Take a breath and think it over. Let me know if you decide to go to the game."

"Okay."

"I'm home. Call me if you need me." And she clicks off.

I look at Lucy and realize, dammit, I forgot to thank Sarah for watching her while I was gone. Alone with my pup, I decided bed is the best place to be.

25

ALEXANDRE

I don't want to bother Callie, but not texting her is like keeping food from a tiger. It's killing me. The waiting is the hardest part, as the song goes. Will she show up at the game tonight? I can't believe I'm sweating a girl showing up for me. This is a first.

I'll admit I can be an ass. But I don't want Callie to share the same opinion. I have to get her to understand things didn't turn out the way I expected. I never intended to fall for her and would never take her for granted. The way I feel about her is different from anything I've ever experienced. But how can I tell her all this when we barely know each other? It seems like it's been longer than a few weeks, but women use these little facts to make larger decisions, and they aren't wrong.

I don't have to touch her for my body to react to hers because the electricity is organic when we're near each other. Without even looking, I can tell when she walks into a room from the way the hair on my neck stands up.

I'm not even out of her driveway and already miss her.

So this is what love feels like. My karma is in trouble if this is the way my ex-girlfriend felt. I've left a path of destruction through women most of my life, and now I will pay the price.

The nerves I feel going into the game tonight are nothing compared to putting myself in front of her, begging for forgiveness. I don't know how to convince her she wasn't a pawn in my chess game to save Peety.

Callie is the first girl I have ever bonded with, and the first girl-friend whose name ever crossed my lips. After just two weeks of dating, she's my obsession.

I have to get her to engage with me so I can explain myself. Given the opportunity, I'm confident I can win her back. I usually get what I want when I want it.

I arranged for two dozen red roses to be delivered to her office, hoping it would make a statement. I've never sent flowers before, but I know red is the color of love. And I know women love getting flowers in public with lots of witnesses.

I suit up and head to the tunnel. The team is psyched up to give the Sharks a good game. With home-ice advantage and some line changes since the last game, we stand a good chance of winning.

We skate onto the ice, and the crowd goes wild. Between the cheering and the music, it's deafening. I warm up, shooting some pucks to Luc in the net.

We take the face-off, and it's a battle from the get-go, not that I expected anything less. As the saying goes, nothing worth having comes easy, but it's especially true tonight.

Checking the stands, I see Callie's seat is empty. Maybe she's just late.

I focus on the game and skate as fast as possible to catch a Shark on a breakaway. I trip him, knowing I'll get called on it, but I have to keep him from getting a shot on goal. I'm sent to the penalty box, and the Maulers have to stave off a goal by our opponents for two minutes.

Ultimately, my play paid off. We got a short-handed goal, and now the game is tied 2-2.

On the ice, I'm back in the hunt. And on the bench, we're sitting on pins and needles if we have a second to think about it. Players encourage each other, and the tablet, playing our game, is passed around so we can review what we did wrong and figure out how to do it differently.

The game ends with us winning 3-2 and Callie never showing up. Normally, I wouldn't care and figure it's over. No big deal, but I'm not sitting this one out. If I have to fight for us, I will. I don't know how to go about it. I have zero experience with chasing women. It's usually the other way around.

We return to the locker room all smiles, and our team's support staff pat us on the back. We shed our smelly gear and hit the showers. As I reach for a towel, there is an Ice under it.

"Fuck you guys!" I yell.

The guys closest to me snicker, and someone yells, "Suck it up, buttercup."

Buttercup, my ass, but I take the knee and chug the shit. No wonder it's called Ice because how it cuts through my throat, and stomach feels like jagged ice shredding my gut. Kinda the way Callie makes me feel by not showing up to my game.

I finally admit, I'm in love. I've got it bad, and she doesn't want me. She's right to be mad at me, but I want to redeem myself. I want my day in her court.

She never returned one text after Boston. I have a day off before we make another trip to Boston for a huge game. This game is important because the winner will have an advantage in the series as the number of games left to play decreases substantially.

I toss around the idea of visiting her at work, so she cannot avoid me. It's stooping low and borders on stalking, but I'm a desperate man at this point.

We all go out to the usual bar to party, and I look around to see if Callie or Sarah are there, and they aren't.

Damn, damn, and double damn.

I party like it's 1999 and don't care how I'll feel in the morning.

We do rounds of tequila shots and pound pitchers of beer. I eat the 'hangover burger' as an ounce of prevention, but the years of conditioning have prepared me for occasions like this when we drink copious amounts of liquor. I stick to beer and tequila and don't make the mistake of mixing tons of shit which will only lead to puking followed by a blinding headache resembling a jackhammer to my skull in the morning.

I'm ecstatic we won, but the celebration feels hollow without Callie here. I don't want the guys to know anything, so I paste on my celebratory smile.

Wyatt comes up and claps me on the back. "Great game. Thanks for that penalty."

"You owe me," I reply because he got the goal from a fresh set of legs on the ice.

"Where's Callie?" he asks, pulling up a chair to sit beside me.

"We had a bit of a falling out."

"She's sweet. I like her. Have you moved on?"

I know he means well. He knows me better than most of the players, even though he's been here the least amount of time.

"I haven't, but I think she has."

"Boston was a bit intense. But it's resolved."

"Yeah, but we're not. I'm working on it."

"Well, I'm here for you."

"Thanks." We clink the necks of our bottles together and finish our beers.

"I'd better be going." I throw a few Benjamins on the table to help with the bar tab and bump fists with Wyatt and other players on my way out.

I don't want to go home to an empty house, but I tell myself it might be for the best.

26

CALLIE

I feel shitty for not going to the game. I work for the organization and had a ringside seat, but I can't face Alexandre. I want to support him, and, like Sarah suggested, he may have an explanation, but I'm afraid to trust him. I don't want to be disappointed again.

What if he lets me down? What if he doesn't love me? I'm older now, and I'm done with the games people play. We want different things, and that's fine. But if all he wanted was a fling, he should have been honest about it, plain and simple, just like my Excel sheets. I like things organized.

Alexandre likes to see where he's going with the puck, and he has a plan for the games due to his years of practice and experience. He knows the players he's up against, and he likes to be forward thinking so there's a disconnect in my mind as to why he misrepresented himself.

Weird dreams plague my sleep, and I wake to a pounding headache and body aches. After a few days of fatigue and flulike symptoms, I call the office to tell them I won't be in. They're not happy about it, seeing as how I just had some vacation days, but what the hell. If I'm sick, I'm sick.

I make myself some black tea and let Lucy out in the backyard. It's so nice outside, so I curl up in a comfy wicker chair on the back porch and drink my tea, enjoying the ambiance of the forest behind my house with evergreen and maple trees.

Lucy wants in my chair, but it's too small, so she sits at my feet. I set my cup on a small end table weathered by two harsh winters and summertime of rain. Even though I bring the furniture into the garage, it still needs repainting every few years.

I text Sarah and find out she's home too, not feeling well, so I'm relieved, thinking this must be something going around. It is flu season.

After a while, my butt gets tired of sitting, and I head inside with Lucy. The screen door slams behind us no sooner than I discover Alexander standing on the front porch.

"Hey, I stopped by work. They said you were out sick. I hope you don't mind me dropping by." He's holding a bouquet of red and yellow roses.

"It's fine," I say, having lost my will to hang on to my anger.

I hold things in until I blow up, and then I'm over what happened. I'm not letting him in my head to mess me up. I need to adjust to a life without him.

I open the door, and his cologne wafts on the summer breeze. The aroma is smooth, just like him when he's in a happy mood, and I regret that we've had our share of disappointments over the past few days.

"How are you?" he asks, awkwardly handing me the flowers.

"Thanks." I instinctively hold the roses up to my nose and inhale deeply. They're perfectly arranged with baby's breath; each stem has a plastic cover on the stem to hold them in an arrangement and preserve them longer. I love getting flowers.

These must have set him back a pretty penny. But then again, he's a multimillionaire, and these probably cost less than a round of golf at his private country club.

"So, how are you?" I meekly inquire.

"Good. I mean, the pressure is on for game six, y'know."

Standing in the doorway, he looks uncomfortable, so I throw him a bone and invite him inside. It's the mature thing to do.

"Thanks." He follows me into the living room, where I move a crystal vase to the mantel over the fireplace. It's high enough so Lucy's tail won't knock it over.

"You fly out tomorrow?"

"Yes, I wish you could go. I realize you have your reasons, and you have a right to be mad at me. I wasn't thinking clearly, and I have a problem with commitment."

"The reason you never say a girl's name."

"Right," he replies merely and stares at his feet as he shifts his weight from one leg to another.

"But you said my name on our first date," I push him for answers. I need closure.

"Right. The guys teased me about it for days. It scared me, it was a slip, or so I told myself. I thought I was safe from falling in love because I saw you to save Peety."

"Hmm." I sit on the sofa and motion for him to sit, too. It's funny how we never really used anything but the bedroom and kitchen before now.

"Look, I want to make it up to you. Just give me a chance to show you I'm for real. I've never been more focused than I am right now."

"What are you suggesting?"

"I'm suggesting we stay together and see where this goes." His crystal blue eyes meet mine, and it's hard to say no.

"Look, I know you can't get off work again, but my sister, Rachel, will be in for the game, and I'd love for you to meet her and my parents. What do you say? Let's do this!"

I could die knowing Alexandre wants me and is here asking for a second chance.

"Oh," I breathe out in surprise. This isn't what I expected.

"Is that good or bad?" His face breaks into a cute grin, and I can't deny his impish grin.

"Maybe I overreacted. You've grown on me, too."

"I'm crazy for you," he declares as he springs the word crazy out. It's so out of character for him to be dramatic. I giggle at how happy my reply makes him. It makes me happy, too.

"That's what you say now. We'll see how you feel in a few months."

"I'm good," he says, reaching for my hands whereby he pulling me up and into his hard chest.

I slip my arms around his neck and close my eyes as our lips meet.

"How sick are you?" he inquires. The concern in his voice is not lost on me.

"Not too bad now," I murmur against his growing beard, the good luck tradition for the Stanley Cup bid.

"Mmm." His kiss deepens, his hand slides under my shirt, and he cups my breast as Lucy rubs against our legs in approval. "Upstairs?"

"You have to ask?"

"No, ma'am." He whisks me off my feet and carries me up the steps for the most incredible makeup sex I've ever had.

Afterward, we lay entwined in each other's arms, marveling at how we navigated the pitfalls that would have sunk most new relationships. I trace the muscles in his arm and caress his body, liking the way his skin feels under my fingers. A girl can get used to this.

"What are you thinking?"

"Mmm. That makeup sex is great, but I hope we won't need to fight to make love like that again."

He lets out a chuckle. "You always surprise me. You come up with some cute one-liners for an accountant's brain."

"Ditto."

"Right." He pulls me closer, and his fingers play with my hair. "I have to leave in the morning."

"I know."

"Do you mind if we just hang out, and watch TV? We can order dinner to be delivered."

"That's fine," I murmur as I settle into his shoulder, but it's too hard, so I lay my head on his muscular chest.

He turns on the TV, and we watch my favorite show even though he hasn't watched any of the previous episodes and has no idea what's happening. I love this final episode so much. I keep replaying it like I would a favorite song.

We talk through the night as if we never had a disagreement. The sun rises, and I send him off with morning sex, knowing I won't see him for two days.

ALEXANDRE IS IN BOSTON, and I'm back at work. I can't wait to see Sarah. Apparently, she's feeling better too.

I find her in her office, and she hands me a cup of coffee from Luke's. It's my favorite crème brûlée latte, but as soon as I smell it, I don't feel so good.

"What's the matter? Is it bad?" She stops sipping hers and stares at me.

"I don't think so. I just don't feel good. I have a feeling I'm not over that bug."

"Hmm. Summer isn't flu season. What's up? Do you need a doctor?"

"No, I'm fine. I think."

But am I? Thinking back, I haven't had much appetite, and the queasy stomach is not going away. Plus, I get light-headed and feel dizzy when I stand up too fast.

"Thanks for the latte. I gotta get work done, see you later." I wave goodbye and head to my office.

My day is easy enough, but Sarah is busy with Logan as we're approaching the June deadline for trades before the NHL draft. There's an opportunity to get a young player named Blake Gibson, a young kid from Minnesota who just graduated from Wisconsin State University and is fast and talented at setting up scoring opportunities for the offensive line.

Alex texts when he gets on the jet, off the plane, and when he's going to the hotel.

I smile. This man must love me.

I cook dinner and talk to Sarah as the game starts, and we're both tuned in. The Maulers start off excellent but fall apart and lose the game.

Shit.

Okay, we can still come back from this. Alex calls me before getting on the plane, and he's not worried too much about the loss. As usual, he takes it in stride.

Good. No stress other than we need to win the home game. The series is tied at 3-3, and we're still on the first series out of three to reach the semifinals of our division. I'm wondering how I will live with the anxiety of making it through three more rounds that would have exhausted the best athletes in the world.

I go to bed and run to the bathroom to throw up. That's weird. Never had that happened before. Came out of nowhere. The wheels in my head start doing the math.

I count days and realize I'm late, as in the infamously late king of late.

Oh, shit.

I look at my birth control pills. Something doesn't look right. I flip the packet over and see the expiration date was two years ago.

Oh no.

I throw on a pair of shorts and a tee shirt and head to the closest 24-hour pharmacy. I buy two pregnancy kits and rush home.

I use one, even though the directions say I should wait until morning.

But I don't have to wait.

I'm pregnant.

I'm not overly concerned as I want kids, and it's so cool to have one at the same time as Sarah. The only question is, what will Alexandre think of it? I have no idea if he wants kids in the future, let alone right now.

I'm meeting his family at the next game. They are in Boston now and will be down for the sixth and potentially our last game. If we don't win this, we're out of the playoffs, and our season is over.

Two huge life events for Alexandre and I are happening now, one of which he doesn't know about, and it takes every fiber of my being not to tell him.

I text Sarah, and she's ecstatic. We're both excited to have kids close in age and wonder if it's a boy or a girl.

27

ALEXANDRE

I'm glad Callie didn't come to Boston to watch us lose. My family is in the stands with some of the other player's wives and girlfriends. We all hang out with each other after the game, but the somber mood makes it a short night.

Rachel and my parents are flying to Maine to see what might be our last game, even though I don't want to admit it to myself. The team won't even talk about it, we all know it's a hard, cold fact. Reality sets in. We may not get to the next round.

I parked my car at the airport because I didn't want Callie to go out of her way. She's been super busy at work, and I plan to see her tomorrow. Coming home to an empty house knowing she's in my life makes it easier and . . . I realized my bachelor days were never going to be permanent after I met her. I'm surprised by this new revelation. I've finally found the one woman who makes me want to settle down, and it's Callie, who I pray will be a part of my future.

～

CALLIE and I join my parents, William and Eva, and my sister, Rachel, for lunch. Girlfriends have all been like ships passing in the night with my parents, and they only met them at a game or family holidays. I usually don't spend my summer in Canada. I love it here and playing with my friends on the golf course or taking wave runners out on the lakes nearby. They are like maple trees, always another one popping up around a corner in the road.

"Mom, Dad, this is Callie."

She extends her hand, and my parents take it, smiling politely and. Dad even stands for the introduction before he lowers himself into his seat again.

We're eating at our pub, which is nothing special but it's convenient.

"Hi, you must be Rachel." Callie hugs my sister.

We're not the overly affectionate type, maybe it's left over from the British connection we have with England, or the fact that it's cold most of the time in Canada, but either way, Callie has the smile that warms the entire room.

"Yes, I am. So, my brother told you about me?" She gives me a look that tells me she's mulling over exactly what tales I've shared.

She's a cute girl with long brown hair that fades into dark blonde at the end. I never understand why she wants to dye her hair when it's not grey. I guess it's a girl thing. These younger kids today are into everything, and her phone is annoying.

I hug my sister because I haven't seen much of her, and we all order. I'm eating healthy but piling on the calories as I'll burn all of it and more off tonight at the game.

Wyatt texts me to ask if I'm bringing someone to his wedding in August as Emily is nagging him for the final count of attendees for the food. There is no need to preplan the liquor as that bill alone will be astronomical.

I text him two or three because my sister might still be in town if that's okay. I figure she will want to visit for the summer. She'll like Emily, giving her time to spend with Callie and keeping her busy so she stays out of trouble. She needs to be looked after even though she's twenty. She's never been on her own, and kids these days aren't as adapted to life as I was, being of a different generation. Plus, it's a bit of the big brother in me.

It's funny that that protectiveness extends to Callie. I've never considered myself the protector, but I like it. Not that the girls can't take care of themselves.

We eat and have a nice meal, but I have to get the hell out of here for a meeting, and I need my nap before tonight's game. Callie and Rachel make plans to hit the mall together. I'm encouraging the friendship but wondering how much my sister will spend when I hand her my credit card.

I probably should have thought this through better, so I recovered from my mistake and gave her a budget that seemed more than fair. Besides, I can't look like a cheapskate in front of my girlfriend.

TONIGHT, I don't think about my family in the stands. It's balls to the wall with a packed house, the media taking pictures of us with long zoom lenses when we walk in, all decked out in our designer suits and leather Ferragamo loafers with no socks.

The night is a struggle from the get-go. The Sharks scored first, which notoriously gives them the advantage in the first two minutes of the game. We throw elbows and make hits, but it's like going over the Wall of China when we take a shot, and we don't have a grappling hook large enough for that. Tonight, we hit the crossbar, it deflects out of play, and we're screwed.

The game ends in a resounding 7-0. I'm embarrassed that my family is here to witness this firsthand. I want to crawl under a rock. The worst part comes after we shake hands with the winning team. We exit the ice, and our fans are booing us like filling the stadium with boos.

I'm so disappointed with the loss and the fans that I want to forget this moment and give my stick away to a kid in the stands hanging over the tunnel—one less reminder. We head to the locker room in silence, and I discover that Wyatt is young, and this was an incredible experience for him. However, he's still impressionable, and being booed is something you'll never forget.

He's sitting on the locker room bench, and I sit beside him, put my sweaty arm around his, still wearing my jersey that stinks to high heaven, and say, "Look, you're young. There will be more opportunities. We might make it next year with a few changes on the team. I heard someone great is coming in for Pete's position. They are trying to rebuild where we need it. So, forget about the fans in the stands who can't take a loss. It's hard but shake it off. Don't let them get you down."

"It's easier said than done," he murmurs, close to tears.

"True, but remember this talk. Let's have some drinks in a quiet place with a few of the guys and commiserate, and then we can work on putting it behind us."

"Sounds good." He sniffles without shedding a tear, and it takes the last bit of strength he has to accomplish this, but he does. We're all champions even if we didn't get the prized procession.

"We played well. It's all we can do. Play your best, go home knowing you worked your hardest, and that's all."

"I'll text Emily that I'll be home late."

I slap his knee as I get up and head to the shower.

The sinking steel ball in the pit of my stomach due to losing is enough to make me sink into a depression filled with booze and pizza. But there is no way to describe the imprint the fans made on me tonight.

And to think that they are the backbone of the team with their money and that I'll have to somehow forgive them for not being kinder when we played our best and came up short.

I hope my few words of encouragement to Wyatt help. The last thing the kid needs is a blow to his ego because I don't want him doubting himself. That would be the very worst outcome of this situation.

Besides, he needs to be happy for his wedding in August, and I'm determined to make sure he's recovered from this. In fact, it's the family event we need to lift our spirits.

That's it. We'll regroup. We'll come back stronger.

28

CALLIE

T he team will not be in the mood to see any of us tonight. I hang out with Rachel, which makes our early afternoon at the mall so trivial and insignificant compared to what Alexandre is going through tonight.

I call Sarah to come over and hang with me as I didn't want to be alone.

"That blew."

"Yes, it did, but Peety is flying out tomorrow, and we're getting…"

"Simon Korhonen in his place. I know. I'm excited, he's incredible, and he'll add depth."

"Yeah, he will. I think we'll have a better shot next year, but one never knows. I mean, some teams go fifty years without getting close again."

"Don't be a Debbie Downer," she adds.

"You're right. I'm just bummed for Alexandre and for me and for the team. And I'm at a loss on what to say about the baby. I had an appointment yesterday before lunch, and it's official."

"Oh, my God." Sarah leans over and hugs me.

"Yeah, right? I'm so excited. It took all my willpower not to say anything before the series ended. Obviously, if it went on to the next round, I'd have to tell him."

"Obviously."

"So, how far are you?"

"I'm in my fourth month."

"I'm only a few weeks, but this little one has me puking in the morning. Good thing I've been able to hide it, but I'm horny as hell."

"That's natural, the hormones." She smiles. "It's so cool we get to do this together. So, you said old birth control pills might be the culprit?"

"Yeah, that, and obviously, my guy has superhuman sperm!"

She choked on the sparkling water I gave her five minutes ago.

"Sorry, that was a good one."

"Is hubby getting that promised vasectomy?"

"Yep, already scheduled. Better now than later."

"Definitely."

"When are you going to say something? I mean, wait until you officially announce it in the second trimester. I have some pregnancy books for you, too. After three kids, there's nothing I don't know."

I chuckle at this because Sarah is always prepared and educated on everything that involves her or her family's well-being. I know I'm in good hands with her by my side for this new adventure.

The only question remaining is . . . what will Alexandre think? Again, hockey changes my plans, and I hate to give him news that changes his life after the huge upset.

I'm sure he's out drinking tonight and might need a few days of bro time and a few hangovers to get over this.

I flip the TV to the sports after-show, and they have some of our players being interviewed. There's no hiding the fact that they are sad and in shock. Even though a loss is always a possibility, they weren't prepared, and no one would be really, but the score made it obvious.

And so did the fans. That bothered me.

"On a different note. Why did the fans boo the players? Who had the most to lose tonight? It's not the fans. They don't get to hoist the Stanley Cup, skate, and make memories with it. The players do so, in my opinion, the fans suck."

"They did. Disappointment is a tough thing, and everyone processes it differently."

"True. I wonder what Alexandre will think about the baby."

"I'm sure he loves you and will adapt."

"Adapt? Sounds so military."

"Hey, it's the same when you have kids, Adapt, Improvise and Overcome!"

I chuckle at her line from an old movie that most people of our age wouldn't know, but her dad was military.

We process the loss of the Maulers and are not looking forward to the aftereffects of it at work.

ALEX and the guys are dropping Peety off at the airport. I assume the name Playoff Pete has fallen by the wayside. He left this afternoon, and Alex told me they Iced him before he got on the plane. Something about the alcohol being strapped into his seat in the car they used to drive to the airport. He's flying out to join his new team, the Ottawa Kings.

"I hope he'll be happy there," I speak into my cell phone as I stare at my computer screen, talking to Alexandre after he returns home. "So, how are you feeling?"

"About the trade?"

"No, I'm more concerned with the team and you over the loss."

"It's hard, but we'll recover. That's what we do."

"I'm learning but can't help myself from worrying about you."

"I'm the one that needs to worry about you. I can take care of myself."

"Yeah, I get it." But there is no way I'm ever going to stop worrying about him, and I agonize over how he'll take the baby news. His family will be leaving so I tell him to take the night with them, and I'll see him after that.

"Oh, by the way, are you going to Emily and Wyatt's wedding with me in August?"

"Is that an invite? Because that sounds more of an after-the-fact question like you forgot to RSVP."

"Actually, I did even better. I RSVP'd two."

"Looks like we have a wedding to go to." I chuckle.

"Alright then. I'll send you a picture of the invite so you can put it on our calendar."

"Hmm. Our calendar. This sounds serious."

"Maybe. I'll see you tomorrow, sunshine. Can't wait."

"Me either."

I'm filled with excitement and dread. What if he's not happy? Are we going to be tried again, and will there be another round with different opinions, or will he disappear when he hears the news?

I have too much on my plate, so I take Lucy for a walk, cook myself a steak dinner for the iron, and have an early night. I can't shake how tired I am, but I'm relieved I know why I'm so tired.

The next day Alex stands me up for a dinner. He's MIA. What the fuck? Is he depressed?

I text Emily. Wyatt is home, so I have no clue where he is and if he's okay. This isn't like him. My mind runs through every scenario of what could have happened to him, and I'm scared. I'm really scared, especially since it's not just me I have to worry about.

I head to his place and let myself in as I've had his key for some time. He's on the couch and asleep with the TV on, snoring terribly.

Oh, boy. I wonder how long this will go on. He's feeling sorry for himself and hiding it from me.

I wake him up and make sure he gets into bed. He pulls me beside him, wanting me to stay, but there is no way. He has scotch on his breath, and I have Lucy. I wonder if he will be responsible enough to make a good father.

But I'll do this on my own if I have to.

I return home and try to sleep. The baby and I need it because it's been a stressful week.

29

ALEXANDRE

I don't know why she puts up with me, but she does. I know there will come a day she'll tell me to clean up my act and that my beard is long and gnarly, but she hasn't complained.

I've been so busy with my family and the game that I should spend more time with her. It's unfair for me to wallow in my misery and bring her down by making her worry. It's because she's authentic and cares so much for me that I love her so much. She's an incredible human, but I'm also scared to take her to a wedding and wonder how long it will be before she wants to get married.

Granted, we've got time, but I'm worldly enough to know it's on the menu for the first time. I'm older and so is she, and we should know what we want out of life and a partner at this point in our lives.

Besides, we're both at the age where we usually settle down. I just don't know how to mention that I love her.

It's Saturday night, and we're returning to our rooftop restaurant to celebrate the season's end and the fact that I'm locked in my contract, so I won't be moving. Thank God. I can't take much more excitement or change right now. Men hate change, and I'm tapped out.

I go to order wine, and she says she's not drinking any. Weird but okay.

"Are you on a diet of some kind?"

"No. I'm fine."

I order a beer, and we talk about the team just a bit, trying to keep our work life from our private life after all the excitement over the trade that almost tanked our relationship.

"So, what's up with you?" She looks like she's excited about something, but her hesitancy is delaying the inevitable news she has to share.

"I don't know how to tell you this, so I'm going to blurt it out, and you take time to process it. Okay?"

"Sure." What can be such a big deal?

"It's big, so I'm warning you. Just know that I'm okay with it."

"You're killing me with the suspense. Tell me," I implore her, holding her hand over the table. "I love you; there's nothing that will change that."

She pauses. "I love you, too."

I smile. Okay, that's a huge step for me.

"So, I'm pregnant. The baby is due in February. I'm sorry, I accidentally used outdated birth control pills, and you must have super strong sperm, but now you know."

I can't catch my breath. I thought saying I love you would be enough excitement for the evening, and I've worked on saying it to her for weeks. But a baby?

"Wow."

"Yeah, right?" Her smile is weak, and I hate to leave her hanging waiting for my responses.

I drain my beer and order another. What a week. Lose the play-offs in the first round, get booed, and become a father in twenty-four hours.

"Well, what?"

"What?" I counter like a jerk. I don't have words. And I don't want to say the wrong ones. I know how hard they are to take back.

"It's okay, take your time. But I'm okay doing it on my own if I have to. I love kids, and I'm happy about it."

My testosterone revs up. "You're not doing it alone. I'm going to be a dad, and that's that."

"You've thought this through?"

"As much as I need to. I'm not leaving my kid for anything, and that's that."

"Okay. I'm just giving you options."

"Consider it a done deal. Let's eat."

I'm abrupt, but I can't think of anything else to say, and I change the subject to the fact my family arrived home safely, and Rachel wants to come and stay with me for a while to get a change of scenery.

She agrees it will give her and Rachel time to spend together and that we'll wait for the appropriate time before saying anything.

Meanwhile, my mother will kill me for having a baby without marriage, and I'm not too keen on it. Kids need stability, and I want only the best for my kid.

"Let's get married," I blurt out.

"No, you can't do that. The baby is no reason to rush into that. I'm the first girl you've ever admitted you loved, and I'm not going to use the baby as a reason to rush into marriage."

"We'll discuss it later." I safely table the conversation knowing how she feels.

But what if I love her and want to marry her even though it's not been years of dating? How do I prove to her that I'm for real and I don't need a baby to make me marry her? She's not going to forget the way I brought up marriage, and I know I have to convince her that it's what two people in love do. The baby makes it a package deal.

WE'RE out kayaking with Lucy, and it's a relaxing morning on the lake. I'll catch up with the guys later. Callie is close to the first trimester and will be showing any day now, and I want to seal the deal.

I can't talk to her about it as she thinks the baby is the reason, and I know how she gets when she has an opinion in her head. Hence the debacle over the trade situation, we both learned that secrets are dangerous and messy.

"We have the wedding later today; we should head back so you can rest beforehand."

"Sounds good."

We paddle together, and I load the kayak and drive back to her house. I figured her house would be best for the kid, but I'm not opposed to getting a place that we pick out together. I think it will make it a fresh start as a married couple, and we can decide what will work best for us with work, my traveling schedule, and a new baby.

A new baby. I wonder what she will be like. Will we take turns getting up at night? Will Callie continue to work? We'll need a nanny if she does due to me being gone so much.

So many questions, and we have time. But I don't want time. I want a commitment and to be settled by the new season. Once the preseason games are over, time flies; the pain and injuries will take their toll, and we'll have a ton of decisions to make between now and when the baby gets here. We still don't know what we're having, but I don't care.

"So we need to start talking about the baby, Callie."

"What do you mean?"

"How do you feel about being a mom? You're excited, but is there anything you are concerned about?"

I drive back to her house.

"I wonder if I can be a hockey mom. I don't know if I can live up to your parents' high standards."

I chuckle. "It's easy. The only difference between a Rottweiler and a hockey mom is lipstick."

She burst out laughing so hard that the water she didn't swallow from her thermos spits out of her mouth, and she quickly throws up a hand to catch it. Then she sputters and coughs.

"Are you okay?"

"That's hysterical," she eeks out.

"Good, you needed the laugh."

"Thanks."

"We also need to discuss logistics and where we want to live."

"You're being too serious," she starts to deflect.

"I'm old-fashioned. I want to be married. I want to live with you and our child, and the clock is ticking. Season will be here soon, and you'll be alone a lot. My sister Rachel will probably want to help, but we need to get things in order. You know I don't like uncertainty."

"That I do. Okay. We'll talk."

EPILOGUE

Callie

"This place is amazing." Callie is wearing a loose summer dress so no one can tell the baby bump will pop out any day. "I never thought I'd be here, though. I mean, talk about pricey."

"Get used to it. This is how we do it. In fact, this wedding is small compared to most."

"I have no idea. I can't comprehend spending over ten thousand dollars to stay here for four days."

"I got it covered. It's not a big deal. You just need to relax and have a good time."

"Should we spend this much money?"

"Relax, babe, I got this."

We pull into Sebago Lake, a resort with high-end, five-star everything. This is where those who have millions of dollars come to the party, use the lake, the golf courses, and the incredible lodges that are so elegant I just want to live here forever.

The decor in the lodge is impeccable, the food is incredible, and late August is beautiful. I just want to relax. And I can as the wedding is tomorrow.

Alexandre is on point with knowing when I need to rest, so I lay down as he goes out to check in with the guys, and seeing as how he's the best man, he needs to make sure things are perfect for Wyatt.

THE NIGHT before the wedding is a huge bridal party dinner in a beautiful event room decorated to the hilt. This dinner is just the wedding party but afterward, the team members who came will all be gathering around the lake for music and more drinks.

I'm standing with Emily, who is radiant as the sun, when she begins to move me to the center of the dance floor. The song *The Whole of the Moon* plays over the speakers.

"What are the odds of that song being played now?"

"No clue," she replies, but there is something behind the grin on her face, only I can't place it.

Her photographer is taking pictures of us, so I stand next to her and pose so she will have a proper picture for her wedding album.

Meanwhile, I notice the team comes forward one at a time, and they are dancing.

Now I wonder what these guys are up to. They can't Ice me as I'm pregnant, thank goodness. There are more and more players coming forward. I don't know all of them all but they infiltrate the crowd of family and friends that are on the dock-type platform that is used for dancing. This is where Wyatt and Emily will take their first dance together as Mr. and Mrs. Hildebrand.

I look to Emily, and she looks to me and then I notice Rachel floating by and joining the guys and then it hits me.

Alexandre comes up to me and lifts me gently in the air as part of the dance and I move with him, imitating what he does and then we're all making the same moves at the same time.

It's a flash mob! I'm giggling and dancing and totally forget that today is the day Emily and Wyatt should be getting all the attention.

Before the song ends, Alexandre kneels in front of me and everyone freezes around us.

"Callie, it's been a ride and a half so far with much more to come. I don't want a future without you. I love you. Will you marry me?"

I take a quick look around and realize this took so much effort on Alexandre's part and that he'll make a great husband and father.

"I love you, too." Tears well up in my eyes. To think he not only listens to me, but he gets me. "Yes."

He slides on a ring that is larger than I ever imagined and to think it fits on my finger. My future husband engulfs me with his huge arms, hugs me a bit too tight and we share a passionate kiss sealing the deal.

"What about Emily and Wyatt? This is their week."

"They gave me their blessing, in fact, it was Wyatt's idea."

"Wow, that's amazing." I'm overwhelmed and these darn hormones bring more tears to my eyes as Alexandre carefully wipes them away.

Emily and Rachel come forward to be the first to give me a hug and the rest of the team congratulates us and pats Alexandre on the back and makes comments that I can't hear.

I do hear someone shout, "Fuck you, Alexandre, no one is safe now that the longest-running bachelor is getting hitched."

"Let's go!" Kal yells as he claps Alexandre on the back rather hard just to screw with him and hands him another beer. He hands one to me and I take it but don't drink. "Why are you not drinking?"

"Not in the mood, I don't like beer."

"Someone get Callie some champagne!"

I take a sip of the champagne so as to not draw more attention to the fact that I'm expecting. I refuse to take any more attention away from the bride and groom this week.

Alexandre pulls me into his arms dropping kisses down my neck before moving down to my breasts which are tender but my nipples are hard, yearning for him to lick them, and touch them. Damn, I'm so horny I'd totally do him behind a tree down the nearest path if I could.

"What are you thinking?" he whispers in my ear. His sexy voice gives me goosebumps.

"That I had given up on love. I couldn't get off the bench, but Sarah pushed me just when then you showed up and now I have everything I ever wanted."

"This is only the beginning, baby."

Follow the Maine Maulers Series as there is a new player on the team, the guys get ready for training camp and preseason is around the corner. . . and love is in the air. Hotter than Puck Book 3 Please leave a review with just a click of a star!

ALSO BY ZOE BETH GELLER

Visit me at my shopzoebethgeller.com

You'll get sneak peaks with my newsletter, bundle deals, and audibles are arriving as well as German books

Tyler: Hooked (Free prequel to the series)

Sin Bin Hockey Series (10)

The Sin Bin Hockey Series

Jackson: Against the Boards

Alan: Between the Pipes

Erik: Fire and Ice

Blayze: Slap Shot

Paavo: The Defender

Spencer: Penalty Box

Isak: Coach

Kaden: Game Time

Liam: The Enforcer

Jake: Roughing

Sin Bin Series Box Sets (3)

The Sin Bin Hockey Series Box Sets

The Sin Bin Hockey Series Box Set Books 1-4

The Sin Bin Hockey Series Box Set Books 5-7

The Sin Bin Hockey Series Box Set Books 8-10

Zoe Beth Geller's Hockey Pond Fan Group

Maine Maulers Hockey Series

Rookie in Love

Jagged Ice

Hotter than Puck

Benched by the Nanny

Puck in the Oven

Pucking the Team Captain

Pucking with the Goalie

Maine Megaladons Football Series

Faking it with the Football Star

The Player's Obsession

Dirty Series-Micheli Mafia

Italian King: A Dark Mafia Romance Book 1

Dirty Vengeance: A Dark Mafia Romance Book 2

Dirty Bargain: A Dark Mafia Romance Book 3

Dirty Born: A Dark Mafia Romance Book 4

Dirty Deals: A Dark Mafia Romance Book 5

Volkov Bratva

King's Promise

Brutal Promise

Sinful Promise

Borrelli Mafia

Free Prequel: Nanny for the Bodyguard

Mafia King: Matteo

ZBG Dark Mafia Fan Group on Facebook

TEAM ROSTER

TEAM ROSTER 2021-22 (subject to change)

C-Kal Kohlman #5, "A" Alternate captain as per Jagged Ice.

C- Jacques Bellare #65

C-Austin Martin, pronounces Maratn #38 is his lucky number

C-Eric Thomas #96

C- Finn Callahan #71

RW-Sean Ian #57

RW-Victor Karlsson "C" for Captain #90,

RW-Alexander Holloway #23

RW-Raymond Frick #73

LW- Wyatt Hildebrand #19 nicknames Hildy, Broomhilda

LW- Albert Bennett #86

LW-Sidney Roy #98

LW-Chandler Ross #49

D-Justin Puljujar #55

D-Colton Cermak #62

D- Simone Korhomen #77

D- Blake Gibson #45

D-Trevor Espisito #41 born April 1

D-Devin Coyle #68

G-Luc McDavid #23 f (or Patrick Roy)

G-Jason McKinney, backup #30 which is Martin Brodeur's number.

RESERVES

F-Greg Coture. #87 for Crosby, his idol as a kid

F-Douglas Wright #8 for Ovchekin

F-Michal Mitchell "#94 M&M" "Candy"

D- Georgiev Laurent #82 "Laundry" and at night "Dirty Laundry"

D-Roy Crug # 71 "Croog" is how it's pronounced

NHL TEAMS FOR THE SERIES

The NHL Team list for the Maine Maulers Series *subject to changes

Atlantic Division
Fort Myers Gators (Jackson: Against the Boards)
Buffalo Blazers
Boston Sharks
Detroit Brawlers
Jacksonville Titans
Ottawa Kings
Toronto Twisters
Wyoming Wolfs
Metropolitan Division
Washington Devils
NJ Bandits
Philly Flames
Carolina Cobras
Montreal Mounties
Nashville Legends
NY Renegades

Central Division

Calgary Oilers

Chicago Blizzards

Colorado Bears (Jackson: Against the Boards)

Dallas Bucks

Pittsburg Rockets

Quebec Pioneers

St. Louis Archers

Vegas Bobcats

Pacific

LA Thunder (Coach: Isak Sin Bin Series)

Edmonton Enforcers

Minnesota Mayhem

Phoenix Diamondbacks (Liam: The Enforcer)

San Diego Defenders

Seattle Whalers

Vancouver Cougars

Vegas Predators

ACKNOWLEDGMENTS

Thank you to everyone who is following me on this journey. I hope you are enjoying this series. Special thanks to my hubby for his support. And as always my besties Mo, Aidy and Aarti and Sandy. You all help me so much as you know the author life and how wild it is!

ABOUT THE AUTHOR

Zoe Beth Geller, a captivator of hearts and a master of suspense, crafting mafia romances filled with unexpected plot twists and thrilling surprises. Her literary journey doesn't stop there; she also delves into the vibrant world of sports, creating enthralling hockey and football romances that never fail to score a touchdown or shoot a hat trick with her readers. A proud resident of Southwest Florida, Zoe cherishes the sun-kissed life alongside her loving family. When she isn't weaving romantic tales, Zoe revels in family get-togethers, enjoying the playful company of her two cherished labs, and indulging in a well-brewed espresso. Each story she writes is a passport to adventure.

Join my sports newsletter for sports!
Email for a link to sign up!
zoebethgeller@zoegellerauthor.com

Fan Groups
Zoe Beth Geller's Hockey Pond
The Dirty Series: Dark Mafia Romances

facebook.com/zoebeth.geller.96

instagram.com/zoegellerauthor

bookbub.com/authors/zoe-beth-geller